FREEDOM
CROSSING

FREEDOM CROSSING

Margaret Goff Clark

AN
APPLE
PAPERBACK

SCHOLASTIC INC.
New York Toronto London Auckland Sydney

ISBN 0-590-42418-1

12 11 10 9 8 7 6 5 4 3 2 1   2   9/8 0 1 2 3 4/9

Printed in the U.S.A.   01

For Vera,
because of her concern for people

Acknowledgments

I should like to thank:

Jeannette Wylie, Supervisor of Social Studies (Retired), Niagara Falls Public Schools, for suggesting the subject of this book and providing information;

John and Margot Owen, present owners of Tryon's Folly, and their son Paul for taking me on several tours through the cellars;

Miriam Harper Macdonald, former resident of Tryon's Folly, for locating the hidden cellar;

Richard A. Fuller, for the use of his report on the Underground Railroad on the Niagara Frontier;

Geraldine H. Hubbard, for the use of her research material on the Anti-Slavery Movement.

Also, for supplying background material and reading the manuscript: Ruth E. Witmer, Donald E. Loker, and Marjorie F. Williams, Local History Librarians, Niagara Falls Public Library; Richard Cary, Jr., Lewiston Town and Village Historian; and Clarence O. Lewis, Niagara County Historian.

Contents

Midnight Visitors

Twelve-thirty! Laura Eastman had been lying awake for nearly two hours, waiting for sleep that would not come. From the oak tree outside her window she heard a screech owl's quavery call. A moment later came the mournful howling of a pack of dogs.

Laura punched her pillow despairingly. Two weeks had passed since she'd returned to the family farm near Lewiston, N.Y., and everything still seemed strange, unfamiliar. The autumn smells of dry leaves and fallen apples, the brisk, cool air of western New York State, and most of all, the hard twang of northern voices, were almost foreign to her after living for four years in the South. Even her own father seemed like a stranger, married to a new wife. And Bert, her brother, had changed most of all.

1

Laura opened her eyes and stared into the dark. Soon she could make out the white lace curtains at the windows. The sight comforted her. At least this room where she had slept for the first eleven years of her life felt like home.

When Laura sat here sewing, and the long rays of the afternoon sun fell across the braided rug, she would feel content for a little while. Then she could forget her homesickness for Virginia and her Aunt Ruth and Uncle Jim. She even could forget her brother Bert's coolness toward her.

Again the dogs howled, this time to the east, toward Lockport and a little nearer the house. As she listened, a new sound reached her ears — a faint tap-tap. She held her breath to hear better. Yes, something or someone was tapping downstairs. But no one was down there. She and Bert were the only ones in the house this Friday night; their father and stepmother had taken a wagonload of apples and potatoes to Saturday market in Buffalo.

Perhaps it was a branch knocking against a window. But there was no wind. How Laura wished their old dog, Prince, were still alive. She had always felt protected with Prince around.

From the room down the hall came the

noise of Bert's bed creaking, and she could hear the shuffle of carpet slippers as he went down the back stairs to the kitchen. So he had heard the tapping, too.

A moment later the outside door opened and there was a soft murmur of voices. Laura sat up in bed. Visitors? At this late hour?

Shivering in the cool September air, she crossed to her door and opened it wider. Someone was in the kitchen talking to Bert, but the voices were so low she couldn't make out what was being said. As she padded down the hall to the stairs, she heard Bert say, "I'll fetch a lamp."

A deep voice answered quickly, "Wait, first let me draw the curtains."

That voice — it had a familiar ring! Laura still wasn't sure who was speaking, but she had the happy feeling that there was an old friend in the kitchen.

Already her bare feet were numb, and she shook with the cold. Hurriedly she returned to her room for slippers and a robe and then hurried back to the stairs, eager to join Bert and the visitor.

Someone had lighted a lamp, for now a glow of light came through the partially opened door at the foot of the stairs.

The deep voice was saying, "This is Martin. Martin Paige. He's had a long, hard trip up from North Carolina."

Laura paused. So there were two visitors.

A chair scraped on the floor and Bert said in his best company manner, "Please sit down, Martin."

The visitor from North Carolina must be someone important for Bert to be so polite. Yet he had called him by his first name; he'd do that only if Martin were a young person.

A soft voice replied, "Thank you, sir."

Yes, the voice was young. Laura felt a familiar pang of homesickness at the sound of the southern accent. She started down the stairs. Bert should know better than to entertain company in the kitchen, even if it was late at night.

Just as she reached the bottom of the stairs, the door in front of her closed softly. As she put out her hand to open it, she heard Bert say, "I hope Laura doesn't wake up."

Startled, Laura pulled back her hand and stood motionless.

The deep voice asked, "Doesn't she know about your — station?"

"No-o," Bert answered slowly. "You know, she's been living down in Virginia with my aunt and uncle for four years — ever since Mother died. She's only been back here two weeks. Pa sent for her as soon as he got married again."

"Oh, yes, you've got a stepmother now. How do you like that?"

"Well, Joel, I like it fine," Bert said earnestly. "Abby — that's what she said to call her — she's good to all of us. And she understands about the — station. It's Laura we have to worry about. Pa says we'd better not take in any fugitives till we find out for sure how she feels."

Laura stood in the dark, her heart pounding. It was Joel Todd who was in the kitchen with Bert! Why had he come here in the middle of the night, and with a visitor from the south? Laura had never before listened in on other people's conversations, but she couldn't seem to move. Why was Pa taking in fugitives? Laura had a suspicion that was too frightening and strange for her to believe.

Bert was still talking. "Maybe she's picked up some southern ideas. Didn't you know you weren't supposed to bring anyone here?"

"Yes," Joel answered. "My pa told me you weren't hiding anyone for a few weeks, but we're desperate. When will your folks be back?"

"Early Sunday morning. They're staying

over with my Uncle Daniel in Buffalo and bringing him back here for a visit."

"Then I'll have to leave it to you," said Joel. "There's a pack of slave hunters in Lewiston asking questions and studying every face that goes by. Somehow they know about Martin."

Now the conversation in the kitchen became painfully clear to Laura. The southerner in the kitchen, Martin Paige, must be a fugitive slave. Pa and Bert — and Joel — must belong to the Underground Railroad that Uncle Jim and Aunt Ruth hated so much. "It's no railroad," Uncle Jim had said. "It's a secret organization for sneaking slaves away from their owners. Those Underground Railroaders have been worse than ever since the Fugitive Slave Law was passed in 1850. I say anyone who helps a slave escape is a thief, because a slave is just as much a man's property as his cow or horse."

Laura's hand strayed toward the doorknob. She shouldn't be standing here in the dark, listening in secret. But if she went into the kitchen, Bert would be cross because she had overheard him. Instead of turning the knob, she raised her hand to the thick plait of sand-colored hair that hung down her back. This wasn't the way she wanted Joel to see her for the first time in four years — in her old pink flannel robe, with her hair skinned back from her face and braided for the night.

Bert's voice broke into her thoughts. "Can't someone else take him in? My Uncle Daniel thinks it's wicked to help the slaves escape. He might kick up something fierce if he saw Martin. And there's Laura — " He stopped abruptly.

Joel Todd said, "Martin may be in some danger if he stays here, but he's sure to be caught if you don't take him in. Pa and I will pick him up before your uncle gets here, and I can't believe Laura would wish him harm, even if she has acquired some southern ideas. She was always kind-hearted."

Laura could hear the amusement in his voice as he went on. "I remember how she lectured me when I caught a rabbit in a trap. I'd set it for the fox that had been raiding our chicken coop. She wasn't more than eleven at the time, but she made me feel like the meanest fellow alive."

Laura remembered well about the rabbit. In those days she and Joel were playmates. He never seemed to mind that she was two years younger than he. What fun they'd had together! Usually Bert had tagged along, as they looked for arrowheads along the bank of the Niagara River or searched the fields and woods around Lewiston for wild strawberries and blackberries. Every fall they had gathered great bags of walnuts and chestnuts and butternuts. Her mother had called her a tomboy, but her father had said, "Let her go. She's healthier than those pasty-faced little girls who never poke their noses out of doors."

That day — the day of the rabbit — they had gone out to the chicken coop behind the Todds' house to gather the eggs. She had gone in first and for a moment, dazzled by the sun outside, she could see nothing, though at once she had heard a high, peculiar whine. Then her eyes had cleared and she saw the rabbit. It was a young rabbit, crouched close to the left-hand wall of the coop, and it was crying like a baby. She could recall how she had run forward to see what was the matter with it, and how she had seen that it was caught in a trap and was badly hurt.

Joel had come up behind her and said, "Go on outside. I'll take care of it."

A moment later the awful crying noise stopped and she thought the rabbit was all right, after all. But when Joel came outside, he told her, "I *had* to kill it."

She had cried then, and had stormed at him. He had stood there and hadn't even tried to stop her when she pounded his chest with her fists.

"Why'd you trap that rabbit?" she demanded.

"I didn't aim to catch a rabbit."

"You shouldn't have set the trap where the rabbit could get in it!"

"I didn't mean to, but we've been losing chickens to a fox."

"You shouldn't trap anything! Traps hurt too much." The rabbit's pain-filled eyes seemed to haunt her. "I hate you!" she screamed, and ran home.

In an hour or so she had calmed down enough to admit to herself that Joel had to protect his chickens from the fox, but she was too proud to go back to apologize.

For several days after that, she hadn't played with Joel. Then he had come to her house with a small, jet-black kitten as a peace offering, and she had gone out with him to look for chestnuts in the woods. That day had been such a happy one. Joel had been so kind to her and they were even better friends than before.

But only a week after that, tragedy had

struck. Her mother had died of typhoid fever and Laura, heartbroken, had been sent to Virginia to live with her Aunt Ruth and Uncle Jim.

"A womanless house is no place for a girl to grow up in," her father had said. "Ruth is childless and she wants Laura."

Now Joel Todd was only a few feet away, beyond the door. She wondered how he looked. It was hard to realize that the deep voice belonged to him, but of course he was seventeen by now, practically a man.

"Martin's worn out. He's only twelve years old." That was Joel's voice. Laura could hear the sympathy in it when he went on, "He came last night to a house on Sixth Street, but one of those slave hunters got suspicious and came around with a search warrant. Martin got out the back way and headed for the woods. That's where he's been hiding all day, poor fellow. They had the dogs on his trail. I don't know how he managed to escape them. I found him not an hour ago, perched in a tree like a bird. This was the closest house, and being outside town, probably the safest. Then, too, the word's gotten around that you have a young southerner living here."

Again Laura heard amusement in his tone.

"I hear she talks like a real Dixie belle. Folks aren't likely to suspect a fugitive would hide out in the same house with a girl from down south." There was a brief silence before Joel asked, "Do you think she'd — talk?"

A burst of anger made Laura forget all caution. Bert and Joel acted as if she were some terrible monster. How dare they talk that way about her behind her back?"

She flung the door open with a crash that brought the three in the dimly lighted kitchen to their feet.

"Stop worrying about what Laura will do!" she cried. "I don't care if Martin goes or stays!"

Dangerous Business

Complete silence followed Laura's outburst. For a moment she enjoyed the look of gaping surprise on the three faces that were turned toward her. She saw Bert's shock change to anger, while Martin's eyes, white in his dark face, rolled toward the back door, as if searching for escape. How small he was, thought Laura, much smaller than Bert, though he was only a year younger.

Joel Todd came toward her, and Laura was amazed at his height and the breadth of his shoulders. He was a man, for sure. Searching his face for traces of her playmate, she noted that his thick brown hair still lopped onto his forehead, but his lean cheeks and jaw were completely unfamiliar. His eyes held no hint of the friendly warmth she remembered. They regarded her coolly as he made a mock bow.

"I see we have an eavesdropper in our midst," he said.

Laura drew in a quick breath and lifted her head defiantly. "All right, I was listening, and I didn't like what I heard."

"Eavesdroppers seldom hear good of themselves."

"I'm not talking about myself," said Laura sharply. "I mean, I'm sorry to find out you and Pa and Bert are breaking the law."

Joel's eyes narrowed. "It's a law that ought to be broken."

"Do you think you know more about what's right than the Congress of the United States?"

"Not ordinarily, but in this case I do. It's a cruel law that says we have to send fugitive slaves back to their masters." Joel pushed a chair toward her. "Here, sit down, so Martin can get off his feet."

Laura considered defying him. He cared more for that runaway's comfort than hers. She glanced at Martin. He *was* tired. The way his knees were sagging, he'd be on the floor in another minute.

She dropped onto the chair. "Please sit down, Martin," she said politely. She kept her eyes on him, trying to ignore Joel's critical gaze. "Martin, when was the last time you ate?"

He cocked his head as if searching his memory. "I had supper night before last, and I found some chestnuts in the woods today."

"Just as I thought!" Laura looked indignantly at her brother. "He's hungry, and you haven't offered him a thing to eat!"

For the first time since she had come into the kitchen, Joel looked at Laura with approval. "Good for you!" he said.

Laura, doggedly honest, replied, "I don't think Martin should be here, but since he is, he should be fed."

Bert seized the poker and lifted one of the two lids on top of the little cook stove.

Joel said quickly, "Don't stir up the fire! The sparks and smoke might draw notice to the house."

Bert put aside the poker. "I didn't think. I'll see what I can find ready to eat." He crossed to the cellar door behind the stove and disappeared down the stairs. Shortly he returned with half a baked ham, butter, and a jug of milk. As he set them on the table, he remarked proudly, "It's a wonder the way my stepmother keeps the larder full. Pa and I never ate half so well when we were batching it."

Laura set out plates and mugs. "Where do you keep the bread?" she asked her brother.

Bert produced a loaf of homemade bread from a cupboard beside the sink.

Joel said in obvious surprise, "You've been home two weeks, Laura, and you didn't know where the bread was?"

Without answering him, Laura began to slice the bread. It was no use explaining, she thought. He'd never understand how it had been in Virginia where Sukey and Della did all the kitchen work and Aunt Ruth merely planned the meals.

Laura had been able to cook as well as a woman when she first went south. But she had rarely helped with the meals during the past four years. Aunt Ruth thought it was more important and fitting for her to learn to sew a fine seam and practice her music lessons, for if she stayed in Virginia, she would marry the son of a wealthy planter and would always have slaves to do the work of the house.

When the food was ready, Bert said, "Time to eat, Martin. You, too, Joel."

Martin said politely, "You're very kind, sir."

Laura was puzzled by the way he talked. He didn't sound like the slaves she had known, but almost as if he'd been to school. When they were seated around the table, she couldn't help noticing that hungry as Martin must be, he didn't bolt his food. He must have had a good master who had taught him well.

"Martin's expected in Canada," remarked Joel, spreading butter onto a piece of bread. "Tomorrow from midnight until two o'clock in the morning his father will wait for him on the Canadian shore north of Queenston. Mr. Paige is already settled in Niagara, on Lake Ontario, with his wife and, I believe, two other children."

Martin spoke up. "That's right, Master Todd. I've got a brother nine years old and a baby sister."

Joel said, "All we have to do is get Martin across the Niagara River tomorrow night."

"How are we going to do that?" asked Bert. "Pa never let me go with him." He sounded resentful. "I should've gone and then I'd know what to do now."

"Don't worry about it," Joel answered. "It's all arranged. A fisherman will let his boat drift downstream tomorrow night just before midnight. I suppose I should say *tonight*, since it's past midnight now, but you know what I mean. At any rate, the fisherman will pull ashore at a certain spot to untangle his lines."

"Where?" asked Bert.

For a long moment Joel's level gray eyes met Bert's. Then he shook his head. "You don't need to know. My father and I will come back here after the moon sets tomorrow night and take Martin there."

Bert pulled back as if he had been slapped. "I wouldn't tell," he muttered.

Joel raised his hand for silence. "Listen!" He quietly pushed back his chair and went to the door where he held his ear close to the crack. Then he moved to the window to tuck the thick homespun curtain more securely against the frame.

In the stillness Laura heard the same howling she had noticed before. Now it came from the south but was closer than ever. Probably those were the dogs that were searching for Martin.

However, Joel didn't seem concerned about the dogs. "I thought I heard someone outside the door," he said as he returned to the table. "I've never seen such a crowd after one fugitive." He smiled at Martin. "You must be valuable."

Martin answered soberly, "My master likes to catch *any* runaway, so's he can take him back and show the other slaves it doesn't pay to escape from him."

Laura felt a cold shudder run up her back. She had heard that runaways were sometimes beaten. Martin was so thin he didn't look able to take such punishment. But tales of masters who beat slaves were rarely true, she reminded herself. Uncle Jim said those tales were made up to get sympathy.

Bert asked, "Are there slave catchers all around Lewiston?" Laura knew he was still trying to decide whether or not to keep Martin.

Joel answered with a brief, "Yes."

Bert looked at Laura and then away. "I wish Pa was home."

Joel frowned and stood up. He paced impatiently the length of the kitchen and back. "Bert, make up your own mind! I tell you I don't know another place I'd dare take Martin tonight. I doubt if it would even be safe to take him out that door. We may have been followed here." He pushed back his forelock. "We've had a fugitive at our house for two days, and we've been watched so close we haven't been able to send him across the river."

Martin looked up with interest. "What's his name?"

"George. That's the only name he'll tell us. He says he was given his master's last name

18

and he wants to forget that. When he's a free man, he'll take a new name of his own choosing."

"Maybe some of the slave catchers are looking for George," suggested Bert.

Joel shook his head. "I don't think they know anything about him. They all ask about a boy named Martin Paige, and they have his description. Of course they'll pick up any black person they see, but right now it's Martin they're hunting."

Bert came to a decision. "We'll keep him. I'm sure that's what Pa would do. I don't know where we'll hide him, though."

Joel looked surprised. "Hide him in the usual place, of course."

"Laura has the room where the trap door is," Bert explained. He kept his eyes away from his sister.

"Oh?" Joel shrugged. "Let her sleep some place else tonight."

Laura seethed with anger. They acted as if she weren't in the room.

"I don't know anything about a trap door in my room. You must've put that in while I was in Virginia. But do either of you realize what would happen to Pa if you get caught hiding Martin?" she demanded.

"We know the law," said Joel. "The fine for

helping a runaway is one thousand dollars, plus maybe another thousand to pay the cost of the slave if he escapes."

"That's two thousand dollars!" Laura gasped. "We might lose our farm!"

"But your pa isn't involved this time," Joel protested. "It's all my doing."

"If Martin's found in our house, Pa will get the blame," declared Laura.

"I'll say leaving Martin here was my own idea," Joel assured her. "Bert's only thirteen, so I figure the law won't hold him accountable."

Laura scoffed. "And supposing you take the blame, where will you get two thousand dollars?"

Joel grinned. "You're right. No one could get that much money from me. Guess I'd have to cool my heels in jail for about six months." His smile disappeared. "No one's going to know Martin's here. That is, unless you tell them."

Laura tried to match the coolness of his eyes, and failed. "I'm no tattletale!" she said angrily.

"Good. Then go up and get the things you want out of your room before we bring Martin up."

Laura stared at Joel in disbelief. Was it

possible he was ordering her out of her own room? Again the feeling of homesickness and aloneness swept over her. She thought of her clothes spread over a chair, her bed with the covers tossed back, the bookshelf over her desk. This runaway slave had no right to her room.

She faced Joel rebelliously. "You'll have to find another place to hide Martin. I'm not giving up my room!"

A Bed by the Stove

Joel exclaimed, "What's happened to you, Laura? You were never hardhearted."

"Come on, Sis," said Bert. "It's only for to-night."

Laura corrected him. "Tonight and all day tomorrow. You won't dare take him away until dark."

Joel agreed. "We'll wait until the moon sets. That's at about ten-thirty tomorrow night. The boat is supposed to pick him up just before midnight."

"How are you going to get Martin to the river when you don't dare take him out the door?" demanded Laura. "That's what you said — you didn't think it was safe to even take him out the door."

"*Now* it isn't safe. The slave hunters are everywhere, but I hope by tomorrow night they'll decide Martin has slipped through their fingers and they'll go back to North Carolina or wherever they came from."

Joel stopped his pacing to stand behind Martin's chair. He put his hands on the boy's bony shoulders. "If they're still around tomorrow night, we can make a dash for the river, if we have to. But now Martin needs a warm place to sleep."

Laura persisted. "You ought to send Martin straight back to his master."

Joel's brows came together, then he took a deep breath as if to control his anger. "Think a minute, Laura, how would *you* feel if someone owned you and made you work in the fields and beat you — "

"Slaves don't feel the way we do," said Laura with conviction. "They — they're like children and they want to be safe and cared for." She appealed to Martin. "Isn't that right?"

"Some slaves feel that way, I guess," he said doubtfully. "But I don't. I want to get all the learning I can and not have any master tell me to come and go and fetch for him."

Laura looked at him in disbelief. "I never heard any slave talk the way you do. I declare, you must be a freedman."

"No, Miss. Except I just set myself free."

Laura was indignant. "You ought to be ashamed of yourself, running away from your master. He'll be worrying about you."

"Yes, Miss." A smile flitted across Martin's thin face. "He's worried, all right. He's thinking to himself that seven, eight hundred dollars just flew right out of his window, and he's going to try to catch up with it." Martin pulled himself to his feet. "Thank you for the supper. I'll be going," he said, starting for the door.

Joel leaped forward and seized his arm. "You're *not* leaving!"

Helpless in Joel's grip, Martin stopped. "I'm just a pack of trouble for all of you."

Laura noted the proud lift of his head. He had spirit, that one. But it would be better if Joel would let him go. He might even be safer out in the woods — she pulled herself up short. She *should* hope that Martin would be caught and taken back to his master. He might be whipped as an example to the other slaves, but after that he would have a home and food and clothes the rest of his life.

Joel pulled Martin back into the circle of lamplight. "If you left here, we'd be in more trouble than we are now. You heard those dogs. They'd find you and bring the slave catchers back here in no time."

"Yes, I sure can hear those dogs," said Martin. "But they don't know where to go. I walked through so many streams today they think their noses are playing tricks on them."

"They're getting nearer," Laura pointed out. "What if they come to the house, anyway?" In her imagination she could see the sheriff marching all of them away to jail.

"We don't have to let anyone in the house unless they have a search warrant," said Bert.

Joel nodded. "And no one's going to issue a warrant before eight o'clock this morning. Seven, anyway." He relaxed his hold on Martin. "Now sit down. Bert, can't we find some other hiding place besides that secret room?"

"I guess so," Bert agreed.

"Let's take a look," urged Joel.

Laura studied Joel's face. He was determined to hide Martin here — nothing she could say would change his mind, and Bert would go along with him. No doubt they thought it was none of her affair. They'd started hiding fugitives long before she came back, and they didn't care a fig for her opinion as long as she agreed not to tell on them.

Bert picked up the lamp. "Let's try the cellar."

Joel and Martin followed him, and Laura,

left alone, was too surprised to protest at their leaving her without a light. She should return to her room, she thought, but she couldn't go back to sleep without knowing where Martin was to stay. Hastily she followed the dim light that was retreating down the steps.

The cellar looked as bleak as a dungeon. The windowless stone walls seemed to move closer as Bert lifted the lamp as high as he could under the low ceiling.

Laura couldn't see a place where a person could hide.

"Maybe in the fireplace?" Bert suggested. He, Joel, and Martin moved across the uneven flagstone floor while Laura trailed slowly after them. The four stared at the black square of the fireplace opening.

"They always look in fireplaces," commented Joel.

"What about the oven?" Bert pointed to a small door set in the fireplace wall three feet above the hearth. Laura could remember seeing her mother open that door and slide in loaves of bread to be baked. Now her stepmother seemed always to use the oven in the kitchen fireplace.

Joel peered inside the bake oven. "I don't know. It's small." He looked critically at Martin. "But so's Martin. Might do. Here, let's see if he fits." He bent his knee so Martin could use it as a step.

Martin poked his head into the opening, but no matter how he turned and twisted, his shoulders wouldn't go through the doorway. Finally he backed out, brushing dust from his head. "I've been in some mighty small holes, but this one's just too tight for me."

"Well," Bert said. "There's still the root cellar."

Laura was amazed that in spite of the danger, Martin seemed to enjoy the search for a hiding place. He looked around the tiny root cellar with an air of satisfaction. Here were sacks of potatoes, carrots buried in sand, and barrels of apples. Before Laura could guess what he was up to, Martin snatched up an empty potato sack and popped it over his head. When he crouched down with his knees jack-knifed against his body, the sack covered him completely. He leaned against the stacked bags of potatoes.

"How do I look?" he asked in a voice muffled by the sack.

Bert turned anxiously to Joel. "What do you think?"

Joel chuckled. "If I hadn't seen him get in, I'd have thought he was another bag of potatoes."

Martin stood up and pulled off the bag.

"I'll stay here." He grinned. "I won't get hungry with all these apples and carrots."

"It's too cold down here," Joel objected. "Damp, too."

"How about the kitchen?" suggested Bert. "If he hears anyone coming, he can get down here fast. I know what he can use for a bed." Thrusting the lamp into Joel's hands, Bert ran across the cellar and took the stairs to the kitchen three at a time.

Laura started after him, but Joel called, "Wait, Laura."

She paused, and he caught up with her.

"Let's not fight with each other about this," he begged. "I can understand how you feel. Up until now, you've only heard the slave owner's point of view for a long time. You ought to listen to the other side of the story."

Laura gave him a level gaze. "I've heard nothing else tonight."

Joel laughed. "You're right."

They climbed to the kitchen, and Martin followed them.

Joel suggested thoughtfully, "There's a book that might clear things up for you — *Uncle Tom's Cabin*. I have a copy you can borrow."

Laura said scornfully, "I've heard of that book. That — that woman who wrote it —"

"Mrs. Stowe — Harriet Beecher Stowe." Joel said the name with a note of reverence.

"She doesn't know what she's talking about. Uncle Jim says that book's made up, all of it. Nobody treats slaves the way they're treated in that book."

"Sometimes they're treated worse."

In silence, Laura began to clear the table. She could hear her brother's quick footsteps overhead in the small attic that was above the kitchen. He soon came downstairs, carrying an old rag carpet.

"This used to be on the floor in Laura's room," he said. "Before she came, our stepmother put down a new carpet. This is old, but it's clean."

Martin took it with a smile, declaring, "A bed for a king." He folded it and laid it on the floor behind the cook stove near the cellar entrance. Dropping onto it, he gave a weary sigh.

Joel looked doubtful. "It looks comfortable enough, but —" With his eyes he measured the distance from the rug bed to the cellar door. "If you hear anyone at the back door, run to the cellar." He glanced at Laura. "I wish — "

Laura knew what he wished, but she couldn't bring herself to offer to give up her room. She had agreed to let Martin stay in the house, and that was more than she should have done. No matter what Joel and Bert said, it was wrong to break the law, and dangerous, too.

She looked down at Martin, already half-asleep, and felt a pang of sympathy for him. He was good-humored and patient — and brave.

Taking a candle, she lighted it from the lamp flame and retreated with it to the door at the foot of the stairs, where she stood uncertainly with one slippered foot on top of the other. She wished she could find words to make Joel and Bert and Martin understand how she felt. No doubt they thought she was mean not to give up her room.

Finally she said, "Well, good night."

Joel and Bert echoed her "good night." But Martin raised his head as he murmured, "Thank you, Miss, for letting me stay."

Laura said gently, "Sleep well."

In her room she set the candle on the dresser. Where was the trap door? she wondered. Full of curiosity, she could not wait until morning to see the hidden room. She lifted a corner of the carpet, rolled it back, and on hands and knees explored the bare floor. There would be a ring or handle of some kind to raise the door, she reasoned, and there would be hinges. Yet, though she examined most of the area of the room, she found no telltale signs. Perhaps it was under the heavy dresser or the wardrobe where her clothes were hung.

At last she smoothed back the carpet. Tomorrow in daylight she might have better success.

Downstairs a door closed. Joel must be leaving. She went to the window that faced west, overlooking the side yard, and watched a tall shadow race across the lawn to the edge of the bushes. Joel's face shone white against the shrubbery. When he moved beyond her line of vision, she hurried to the front window in time to see him turn onto the Ridge Road toward Lewiston. Once he had been her best friend, she thought as she knelt with her arms on the sill, but now they were miles apart — farther even than when she had been living in Virginia!

Laura sighed and got to her feet, but just before she dropped the curtain into place, she saw someone move from the bushes on her left and hurry lightly down the road toward Lewiston. Someone was following Joel!

The Secret Room

Laura ran out of her room and almost collided with Bert at the top of the stairs.

"Someone was hiding out by the road!" she whispered. "I saw him run after Joel!"

"I'm not surprised," said Bert calmly. "And you don't need to whisper. No one's in the house but Martin and the two of us."

Laura shook his arm. "Don't you understand? If you take the short cut through the woods you might be able to catch up with Joel and warn him."

Bert went into his room and sat down on the edge of the bed. "Don't worry. If someone's following Joel, he knows it. He doesn't miss a thing." Bert kicked off his slippers and stretched out on his back.

Laura looked down at her brother, amazed at his indifference. "You're a mighty poor friend, Bert Eastman! Joel may be fighting for his life this very instant."

"I'd be a worse friend if I followed him." Bert raised on one elbow and scowled at Laura. "If those slave hunters saw me coming through the woods after Joel, they'd *know* we were up to something. Next thing, they'd come back here and tear this house apart until they found Martin."

"You care more about that — that *darky* than you do about Joel. I declare, you must be touched in the head!"

In the dim light Bert's face was an unfamiliar mask with shadows where his eyes should be. "I forgot what it was like to have a big sister bossing me around," he remarked. "Can't say I enjoy it." He turned onto his side with his back to her.

Laura drew in a quick breath. It didn't seem possible this was her young brother talking so impudently.

"You won't have me bossing you around much longer." To her annoyance she heard her voice quaver. "Just as soon as I can, I'm going back where I'm wanted. Uncle Jim and Aunt Ruth begged me to stay!" She whirled around and walked swiftly to her room, closing her door firmly behind her. Tears of hurt and anger filled her eyes, but she rubbed them away with her arm. She refused to cry over Bert — or Joel Todd, either!

Laura awakened to a sound of tapping. Tapping — again! In a half-daze she thought, Oh, not another runaway! Then as her senses cleared, she realized the tapping was on her own door. She sat up, pulling the bedclothes up to her chin. The door inched open and Bert poked his head through the opening.

"Good morning," he said, coming into the middle of the room. For a moment he was silent, shifting from one foot to the other. Then he said awkwardly, "I'm sorry I snapped at you last night about being bossy."

Laura leaned back against the headboard of the bed and replied stiffly, "That's all right." She glanced up at him, noticing with surprise how the sunlight shone on the light fuzz on his upper lip. Her little brother was gone forever. It wouldn't be long before he would be shaving, though he was only thirteen. Already he was broader in the shoulders and taller than she was.

Suddenly, seeing him standing there, she was reminded of the time long ago when, having misbehaved at the supper table, she had been sent to her room with her meal only half-finished. Bert had come up that night, bringing a smuggled cookie, and had sprawled companionably on the floor beside the rocking chair where she sat in lonely misery.

"We had applesauce, too," he said, "but I couldn't save any of that for you. I couldn't put that in my pocket."

With her mouth full of cookie, she asked, "Is this yours?"

"Yes."

She held out what remained. "Here. You didn't have to do that."

He shook his head. "You eat it."

That's the way it had been between them. She had once heard her father comment, "Bert and Laura may quarrel, but as soon as one of them's in trouble, they come together, thick as thieves!"

Now that closeness was gone, and Bert was little more than a tall stranger. Indeed, it scarcely seemed right that he should be in her bedroom.

A fragrant scent wafted through her open door.

"I smell sausage!" she exclaimed. "Have you had breakfast?"

Bert grinned. "Not yet. We have a cook this morning. Martin used to be a kitchen boy."

Laura reached for her robe at the foot of the bed. "I'll dress and be down shortly."

Bert started for the door and then stopped abruptly. "I see you've been looking for the trap door," he remarked. "Did you find it?"

Laura followed his gaze to the wrinkled carpet. "No, I didn't."

Bert knelt and rolled back the carpet. He pointed to a section of bare floor between the bed and the doorway. "There it is."

Laura joined him, buttoning her robe. "I looked there and I couldn't find it. Of course I only had a candle for light." She studied the floor boards. "I still don't see any trap door."

Crouching, Bert slid his fingers into a small crack. To Laura's amazement, he lifted out an oblong section of the floor, revealing an opening large enough to admit a man's body.

"Well, for pity's sake!" she said.

"Clever, isn't it?" Bert looked pleased at her surprise. "We didn't want a ring or handle that would show. Hinges would be a giveaway, too, so we got this idea. This section rests on a frame that holds it up. And nobody notices this little room from downstairs because the hall closet is under it. We just lowered the ceiling in the closet."

Laura peered into the hole at the coffinlike chamber below. It was only three or four feet deep — a person couldn't stand in it — and it was wide enough for only one or two people.

"How long do they hide in there?" she asked.

"All day. Sometimes longer."

"I should think they'd suffocate."

"We drilled holes along the side. See?"

She shuddered. "It must be dark as night when you put the cover on. I'd hate to stay in there. A person couldn't even read to pass the time away. Of course," she added, "your fugitives can't read, anyway."

"Usually they can't, but Martin can."

"Nonsense. Did he tell you that?"

"Yes, said Bert. "And besides, he read to me from a newspaper." He replaced the trap door. "Hurry up. Martin must be starved. He's been up for over an hour. He got the fire going and took a bath before I even went down."

"He doesn't have to wait for me," Laura said, with a return of yesterday's annoyance. She realized, too, that her head was aching. No wonder, with the little bit of sleep she'd had the night before.

"He won't eat before we do," answered Bert.

"If you'd get out, I could dress," she said, her voice sharper than she intended.

Martin looked like a different boy this morning, Laura found. Clean, and wearing a pair of Bert's outgrown pants and one of his old shirts, he was presiding at the cook stove. Three pancakes were browning on the griddle, and on Laura's arrival, he removed crisp sausages from a pan at the rear of the stove and placed them on a platter.

"Morning, Miss Laura," he greeted her, ducking his head shyly. "Breakfast's ready."

"Come on, you sit down with us, Martin," urged Bert.

Martin shook his head. "I'll eat by the stove where I can turn the griddle cakes," he answered.

Laura knew that he was not accustomed to sitting down with white people. She had been surprised when he had consented to sit at the table with her, Joel, and Bert the night before. Uncle Jim's slaves always ate by themselves. Probably last night he had been too tired and hungry to object.

"It's awfully dark in here," she remarked. "Why don't you open the curtains?" A lighted lamp glowing in the middle of the table made a small area of light in the dimness. She briskly pulled back the curtains, letting in a flood of sunlight. "There, that's better." Silence was her only answer and she became aware that the two boys were looking at each other and that Martin had backed against the wall behind the stove. "Oh," she said. "You're afraid someone will look in the window and see Martin."

"That's right," Bert agreed.

"But a covered window in the daytime really looks suspicious," she pointed out.

Bert nodded to Martin. "She's right." He turned down the lamp and leaning over, blew it out.

Slowly Martin returned to the stove, but Laura noticed he kept his eyes warily on the window.

Eating the delicious pancakes and sausage, with Martin hovering nearby, ready with a fresh serving, made Laura feel as if she were back in Virginia at Aunt Ruth's. She relaxed and almost forgot the danger that hung over all of them.

With a spoon she caught a trickle of maple syrup that was running from the spout of the pewter pitcher. Absently she licked the spoon, savoring the sweetness. Maple syrup was so much tastier than molasses, she thought. How long it had been since she had helped Pa at the sugaring off. That was always such fun, stirring the sap in the big kettles, early in the spring when the snow was still on the ground — but she wouldn't be here for that. Long before spring she'd be back in Virginia.

"Martin," she said. "I hear you know how to read."

"Yes, Miss. My pappy taught me. I can write, too, but spelling gives me some — "

Laura looked up, wondering why Martin didn't finish what he was saying. She saw that his eyes, wide with terror, were fixed on the window. Instantly Laura guessed what had happened. He had seen someone outside.

No one was in sight now, but a sharp knock sounded on the back door.

A Surprise Visit

For a few seconds the three in the kitchen remained frozen. Then Martin, the first to move, wrenched open the cellar door and disappeared down the stairs. To Laura's relief, she saw that he had carried his plate with him.

Bert cast a hasty glance around the room, and called out, "Just a minute!"

Laura wished she could hide, but no doubt their visitor had already seen her and would wonder why she had left. As for Martin, at least he had been farthest from the window, and being black, had been less noticeable.

Of course the person at the door might even be Joel Todd. This morning she was willing to have him see her, since she was wearing a starched blue housedress and her

41

hair, smoothly brushed, was pulled back and tied with a blue ribbon.

Bert's eyes questioned her and she answered for the benefit of listening ears, "I declare, Bert, you're the slowest-moving boy. Whoever's at that door will think we're still abed."

She noticed too late that the cellar door was ajar, but she did not dare close it, for Bert was already drawing the bolt on the back door.

A tall, spare, middle-aged woman with wispy gray hair stood in the doorway. Laura, recognizing their nearest neighbor, from a quarter of a mile up the road, did not know whether to be glad or sorry. She would have preferred Joel, but at least Mrs. Fitch was better than a slave catcher. Still, she did have a reputation for being a busybody.

Bert said with false heartiness, "Good morning, Mrs. Fitch. Come in!"

"Good morning, Bert. Morning, Laura. You'd better pay attention to those griddle cakes."

Laura ran to the stove, where a curl of smoke was arising from the griddle. The pancakes were as black as the stove. She stacked them with the spatula and dumped them into the fire.

"Wasteful," commented Mrs. Fitch in her brisk voice. She set a small basket on the table. "I brought you some biscuits. Thought I'd better see how you two young ones were getting along without your father and step-mother."

"We're doing all right," said Bert.

"Just fine," Laura assured her. "And thank you kindly for the biscuits. Can I fix you some pancakes?"

"Land's sake, no! I had breakfast over an hour ago. It's past eight o'clock, you know." Her eyes were busy, swooping over the entire room, lingering on the untidy stack of dishes beside the sink, left from their middle-of-the-night meal. "I won't hold you up," she said. "You must be in a hurry to get on with your chores." She looked pointedly at Bert. "I don't suppose you've taken care of the horse?"

"Not yet," Bert admitted.

What a pity Mrs. Fitch had chosen this morning to visit, thought Laura. It wasn't like Bert to neglect the horse, for he was fond of the lively young filly he had named Sally.

Mrs. Fitch's expression showed clearly that this was just what she had expected. "Humph," she said, "you'd better get a hustle on. I know how particular your father is about having the animals fed and watered right on time, and I 'spect he left you a few other jobs to do, besides."

"That's right," Bert replied. "I have plenty to do to keep me busy all day and half the night."

Still Mrs. Fitch didn't go. "I notice you haven't started school yet, Laura. Are you going back, or do you think fifteen is too old for school?"

"I haven't decided yet," said Laura. When she had come north she had expected to enroll at once, but she had come down with a bad cold the day after she arrived. As the days had passed, she had begun to dread going to a school that would be strange to her. After her long absence, she would know few of the other students. And now that she had made up her mind to return to Virginia, there didn't seem to be any reason to start classes here.

At last the door closed behind Mrs. Fitch, and Bert grinned his relief. "She'll be reporting to Pa what a poor farmer I am."

Laura had other worries. "By the way she stayed around and stared at everything, I'm afraid she's suspicious. Do you think she'll go to the sheriff?"

"She might." Bert ran his fingers through his hair in a worried gesture. "But on the other hand, she's always interested in other people's business." He pulled open the door to the cellar. "Come on up!" he called.

Martin bounded up the steps, smiling broadly. "I was all ready for company," he said. "I had the sack on." He looked at the stove. "Sorry about those pancakes. I'll fix some more."

"Never mind," said Laura, "unless you or Bert want more."

"No more for me," said Bert. "I'm going out to look after Sally and the chickens." He paused with one hand on the latch. "Martin, when I come in, we're going to look for another hiding spot for you. The cellar's the first place the slave hunters will go."

"But if I'm in the potato sack, they won't find me."

"They might. Some of those fellows have had a lot of practice hunting for fugitives. We have to hide you better."

While Bert was caring for the livestock, Martin poured hot water into the washtub and scrubbed his clothes.

Laura went up to make her bed and straighten her room. She was sure that Bert wished she would offer to let Martin use the secret room, but she was not going to do that. If he wanted it, let him ask again!

Before long, Bert returned from the barn, and Laura heard the two boys climb the back stairs and enter Bert's room.

Had Bert locked the back door? she wondered. Rather than ask him, she went down to check, leaving her bedroom work half-finished.

The door was bolted. No doubt about it, Bert was more responsible than he used to be. Laura turned around and surveyed the kitchen. Martin's clothes were drying on a rack behind the stove. Dishes from breakfast and the night before littered the table and work shelf. She wrinkled her nose in distaste at the dirty dishes.

"Oh, well," she said to herself. "I might as well get started." Bert was too busy getting Martin settled to think of kitchen work, and besides, he had the outside chores to do. Once again, she wished she were in Virginia. A housewife there was busy enough, heaven knew, with planning the meals and seeing to it that the slaves did what they were supposed to do, but at least she and Aunt Ruth hadn't had to clean up the kitchen. The people in the south had a different way of life. They had more time for music and books and parties.

Laura carried the butter and milk down to the cellar. She soon located the place where they belonged — a box that was set into the cool dirt and flagstone floor. This box was only for the day's supply of perishable food, she recalled. The big cans of milk and the crock of butter were stored outside in the springhouse where cold running water kept them fresh.

She climbed back to the kitchen, put water on the stove to heat, and began to scrape and stack the dishes. When her mother was alive, Laura had enjoyed helping in the kitchen. Now, doing the once familiar tasks, she found herself humming.

Where did Abby keep the dishpans? Laura wondered. She was startled to realize that this was the first time since she had come home that she had cleared up after a meal. Abby hadn't asked her to do a thing.

Alone in the kitchen and busy with her hands, Laura shook off some of the gloom that had weighed her down since her arrival in the north.

Abby had been kind to her from the first. Funny she had never married before — she must be all of thirty. Being warmhearted and quite pretty, you'd have thought some man would have noticed her.

Well, Pa had noticed. It was easy to see he

thought she was perfect. He was always making little jokes and looking at her to catch her eye and watch her laugh. Abby made all of Pa's favorite dishes, and Laura had several times seen her give him a quick kiss when he came in from the barn or the fields.

Seeing them together and how happy they were had made Laura feel more lonely than ever. She wondered how Abby felt about the Underground Railroad. Probably she was in favor of helping the slaves. She seemed to think everything Pa did was just right.

Laura found the dishpans on the bottom shelf of the cupboard and scooped soft soap from a crock into one of them. As she lifted the teakettle from the stove, a distant sound made her pause. The dogs were howling again! They were still searching for Martin!

An Educated Slave

Laura put the teakettle back on the stove. Upstairs, all was silent. Were Bert and Martin listening to the dogs, too?

Running to the foot of the stairs, she called, "Bert! Where are you?"

"Bert's answer came from the spare bedroom. "Come on up!"

She found him standing alone in the chamber that lay between her room and the back stairs.

"Where's Martin?" she asked.

"See if you can find him."

"Bert, this is no time for games! Did you hear the dogs?"

"I did, and this isn't a game. I want to know if Martin's in a good hiding place."

"Oh, all right." Laura turned slowly in the middle of the room. "Under the bed?" She lifted the edge of the white bedspread. No one.

"That would be too simple," Bert said scornfully.

"Then there's only the wardrobe." Laura opened the door of the tall cabinet that stood against the south wall. A strong smell of camphor almost overwhelmed her as she faced the close-ranked row of winter clothes hanging on the rack. Backing up, she knelt to look at the floor of the closet and saw a scuffed pair of shoes and above them a pair of thin ankles.

Laura stood up. "His feet show. You ought to put a row of shoes under the clothes."

Bert scowled, annoyed as usual at being told what to do.

Martin's dark head poked out from the stored clothes. "That's a good idea, Miss Laura. There's some shoes back here in the corner." He disappeared again to rummage on the floor of the wardrobe.

Laura felt worried. It had been too easy to find Martin. "Can't you do better than that?" she asked Bert.

"I didn't say it was a perfect place to hide him," Bert said. "But it was the best I could think of."

"How about the attic?"

"Abby cleaned it out. You couldn't hide a mouse in it."

Martin backed out of the wardrobe and began to place shoes in a row beneath the hanging garments. He paused and lifted his head as a dog howled again in the distance.

"Listen to those hounds!" He shook his head and went back to arranging the shoes. "If they ever catch up with me, they'll tear me up in little pieces. They'll be so mad at all the work I made for them."

Laura was struck with a new thought. "How can those dogs track you? They'd have to sniff something you wore before they could follow your trail."

Martin looked up. "I guess after my master hired a slave catcher, he gave him an old shoe of mine or something. He's a powerful determined man."

"But there are *lots* of slave hunters in Lewiston looking for you. That's what Joel said. Your master couldn't have hired all of them."

"Maybe they read the posters. I saw some when I was coming here — they're nailed up on barns and trees. They tell what I look like and they say my master will give a big reward to anybody who catches me."

Laura was still puzzled. "How do the slave catchers know where to search?"

Bert said, "*Everybody* knows runaway slaves head for Canada."

"There are lots of other places on the border besides Lewiston," Laura pointed out.

"Look, Laura, there are *hundreds* of fellows making a living as slave catchers, especially since the Fugitive Slave Law was passed, and they just sit themselves down at a border town and wait till they see a black face." Bert sounded impatient. "Lots of them don't care whether the person they catch is a free man or a slave. They'll ship any blacks down south and sell them like cattle."

"But Joel said the slave catchers are looking for Martin. How do they know he's here?"

Bert exploded. "How do I know? Ask Joel! Maybe someone recognized Martin when he was on the way here."

Laura bristled. "You don't have to be so cross just because I ask a few questions." She sailed out of the room before Bert had time to retort.

As she went down the hall to her room, she heard Bert say to Martin, "I'd better get outside again. I still have chores to do."

It was a day for interrupted tasks, thought

Laura. While she finished straightening her room, she puzzled over her newly acquired information on the slave catchers. She wasn't sure whether or not to believe Bert and Martin. She thought it was natural for a slave owner to try to get back his property, but it surely wasn't right for people to catch a freedman and sell him down south. Then she remembered a black who had been bought by the owner of the plantation next to Uncle Jim's. He had insisted that he was a freedman and that he had been picked up by a slave catcher. No one had believed him, and for all she knew, he was still working for his new owner.

Downstairs she heard a rattle of dishes, reminding her that she had left the teakettle singing on the stove and the soap ready in the dishpan. It didn't seem likely that Bert was washing the breakfast dishes, but who was?

The kitchen was empty and the rattling sounds came from the pantry, where Laura discovered Martin at work with the dishpan set up on a shelf.

He turned around as Laura pushed open the door. "I came in here so I'd be out of sight," he said. "If someone comes to the back door, I can run out through the dining room and up the front stairs. If they come to the front door, I can hurry up the back stairs." His smile asked approval of his foresight.

"It's a good plan," Laura agreed. "And it's good of you to do the dishes. Did Bert ask you to do them?"

"No. He's still outside."

Laura leaned against the cupboard. Here was a chance to find the answer to some of the questions that were plaguing her.

"Martin, you said your father taught you to read. Isn't that unusual? The slaves I knew down in Virginia couldn't read or write."

"Yes, Miss, it's unusual, all right. It's against the law to teach a black man to read, but my pappy once had a kind master who taught him and let him have books to read. My pappy," he said proudly, "used to keep the account books for that master."

Laura studied Martin's face, trying to decide if he were telling the truth. "My Uncle Jim said it wasn't any use educating a slave," she said.

"That's what Mr. Spencer, our new master, said, too."

"What happened to your father's master, the good one who taught him to read?"

"He died, and all his slaves were sold to Mr. Spencer."

The back door opened and Laura and Martin jumped. Laura opened the pantry door a crack.

"It's just Bert," she said, relieved.

Bert joined them in the pantry. "You shouldn't be downstairs," he told Martin.

"I'm almost finished," Martin reassured him. "Then I'll go up and stay there. Sitting and waiting, that's the hardest thing to do."

"I'm going out to dig potatoes so I can keep an eye on the road," Bert said. "But first I'll find a book for you."

"I'd like that." Martin chuckled. "My master sure would be surprised if he knew a white boy was offering me a book to read. He sure hated to see a slave reading."

Bert spoke up. "Show Laura what your master did to you for teaching one of your friends to read."

"I don't think I ought to do that, Mr. Bert," objected Martin.

Laura's curiosity was aroused. "What do you mean?"

"Well," said Martin hesitantly, "Mr. Spencer said he'd teach me to forget how to read."

Laura was still mystified. "I don't understand."

Bert attempted to explain. "Pa says slave owners think it's harder to keep a slave in his place if he can read and write. He told me about an educated slave named Nat Turner who led an uprising against white people. Ever since that happened, plantation owners are more scared than ever of letting their slaves learn anything."

"I've heard about Nat Turner," said Laura. "But I don't see how Martin's master could make him *forget* how to read."

"Show her, Martin," Bert insisted.

Martin shook his head, but Bert unbuttoned the top three buttons of the boy's shirt and pulled it down from his shoulders. Turning Martin around so Laura could see his back, Bert said grimly, "What do you think of Mr. Spencer's teaching?"

Laura gasped. Martin's back was crossed with long scars that she knew must have been caused by a heavy whip.

The Slave Catchers Come

Deeply upset by the sight of the scars on Martin's back, Laura went up to her room, leaving him still at work in the pantry. She took out her needlework and sat in her rocker by the west window. She was sewing a ruffle on the bottom of a green cotton dress to make it longer, for she had decided it showed a little too much of her ankles. But she was not thinking of her sewing. Her mind was in a turmoil over the happenings of the past few hours. It seemed that her world was turning upside down.

At Uncle Jim's she had seen only gentle treatment of slaves. His slaves were never beaten, and if they were ill, Aunt Ruth cared for them as if they were her own children. Laura wanted to believe that all plantation owners were as kind as the Montgomerys.

But Martin's scars were proof that this was not true. Perhaps, she told herself, he was lying and had been beaten because he had done something bad, like stealing. Yet even that wouldn't be a reason for so cruel a beating. Besides, she believed Martin had told her the truth. As she puzzled, she rocked furiously, and her sewing lay in her lap.

The clock on the front-stair landing chimed nine. The slave catchers had had time to get a warrant to search the house. Since no one had appeared, Laura tried to convince herself they had decided not to come. At any rate, Bert was outside watching the road, so he would stop anyone who approached. But every time a dog barked or hoofbeats sounded on the road, she stiffened in alarm.

She wondered if Joel would come this morning. Probably not, for he wouldn't want to draw attention to their house. She liked his appearance since he had grown up. He wasn't exactly handsome, but he looked to be the kind of person you could trust. It was a pity he had such strong ideas about slavery.

Deep in thought, Laura was startled to hear voices in front of the house. She ran to the front window and looked down at a group of men, one of whom wore a sheriff's badge. The bell in the front hall rang as someone tugged on the bell pull outside the door. Then Laura heard the doorknob being tried.

"It's locked," one of the men shouted. He stepped back and stared up at the house.

Laura dropped the lace curtain, hoping he had not seen her gazing out. She was horrified to realize that these strangers would have walked directly into the house if the door had not been locked. Again she wished Prince were alive. He would never have let them into the house.

Through the thin curtain she could see the men talking together, apparently trying to decide what to do next.

Bert came around the corner of the house on the run, with the wide-tined fork that he used for digging potatoes still in his hand.

"Good morning!" he called out.

The men whirled around.

"Oh, good morning, Bert." The sheriff coughed nervously. "We've come to look through your house. Hope you have no objection."

"Why did you come?" asked Bert. Laura was amazed at his unruffled manner.

"You know well enough," one of the men growled.

Bert turned to him and Laura could see the surprised lift of his eyebrows. She had not guessed her brother was such an actor.

The sheriff said politely, "We're looking for a runaway slave, and some people think Joel Todd brought him here last night."

"I heard there was a fugitive around," said Bert. "Of course you can search the house." He paused. "I guess you have a search warrant."

"That we have," said one of the men, a young fellow with a crest of black hair. "I'll bet you're sorry to hear that. Show him the warrant, Sheriff!"

"Don't hurry me, Walt." The sheriff pulled from his pocket a paper which Bert studied carefully.

The men were getting restless. The young man called Walt pushed his face close to Bert's. "You know a search warrant when you see one. Now get that door open!"

Bert said politely, "If you'll wait here, I'll let you in. I only have the key to the back door with me." He fished a large key out of his pocket and held it up for all to see.

"Since when do you lock the doors when you're working in the garden, Bert Eastman?" asked one of the men.

"Seemed like a good idea, with a fugitive

loose in the countryside," said Bert. " 'Specially since my sister's alone in the house."

Walt said, "Oh, yes, your sister! I heard she came back here from down south. Hear she's a good looker, too."

Laura blushed, glad that she was upstairs behind the curtain. What a rough lot those men seemed to be — all except the sheriff. And yet they were acting according to the law, trying to catch a runaway and return him to his master. It was hard for her to remember that last night she had thought it would be best for Martin to be caught and returned to his owner.

As Bert started around the house, one of the men called after him. "Not so fast, Bert! I'll go with you just to see there's no monkey business. Spread out around the house, men, and make sure that darky doesn't climb out of a window."

Laura was shocked by the hate in the man's voice. Why he sounded as if he thought Martin was a criminal! She ran to the spare room. Martin was not in sight. She opened the wardrobe, and whispering, "Are you in there?" pulled aside the clothes until she could see Martin's face. His wide, frightened eyes peered out at her. "I'm here, Miss Laura. Don't let them catch me! Please!"

"Stay quiet!" she cautioned. She closed the wardrobe door tightly and hurried back to her room. Downstairs the front door crashed open, and booted feet sounded on the hall floor.

"The cellar first!" someone cried out.

The men thudded through the house like a herd of buffalo. Less than five minutes later, the footsteps pounded up the cellar steps and began to travel through the rooms on the first floor. Now and then Laura heard the crash of a chair being overturned.

Standing in the middle of her room with her fists clenched, Laura's anger and fear grew with every passing moment.

Judging by the noise downstairs, those men wouldn't miss a corner of the whole house. In no time they'd find Martin and take him away. She kept seeing his eyes and hearing his voice begging her not to let him be caught.

Someone was on the back stairs, running lightly, taking the steps two at a time. Still Laura could not move. The quick steps hurried down the hall to the spare room. A moment later they reached her door, and to her amazement, Bert rushed into the room, pulling Martin after him. Without a word he flung back the carpet and knelt to lift the trap door.

A man's voice came clearly up the back stairs. "He isn't down here, men! Take the next floor!"

Bert had the trap door open and was pushing Martin into the opening as the men swarmed up the stairs. Laura heard them go into Bert's room and from there into the attic over the kitchen.

Now Bert had the trap door in place and was pulling the rug smooth, while the searchers prowled about the spare room, tapping on the walls and even opening bureau drawers. What did they expect to find in a drawer? Laura wondered in amazement.

The loud voices carried easily into her room.

"Look under the mattress!" one said. "I heard about a darky who crawled under a feather bed. Only way they found him, the feathers tickled his nose and he sneezed."

"Look in that closet over there," said another man. "That's a dandy place. Look good behind those clothes."

Bert pulled Laura's rocking chair into the middle of the room, directly over the trap door, and shoved her into it, none too gently.

"Sew!" he commanded.

Now the searchers were at the door of her room.

Moses Is a Woman

Seeing a girl seated in a rocking chair, with her sewing in her lap, the men stopped in the doorway.

The young man Laura had noticed outside her window, the one the sheriff had called Walt, was the first to recover.

"Well, look who's here!" he exclaimed, swaggering across the threshold. "It's young Miss Eastman herself, and just as pretty as I heard she was!"

Laura's anger rose to the boiling point. She had no objection to being told she was pretty, but the young man's tone was so familiar that she felt insulted. Bert should put him out of the house! But Bert had disappeared.

Without rising from her chair, she demanded angrily, "What right do you have to come into my room?" Even to her own ears, her accent was as pronounced as her Aunt Ruth's. "No *southern* gentleman would think of doing such a thing!"

Walt did not move. "Well, aren't we high and mighty!" His eyes, bold and mocking, never left Laura.

The sheriff stepped forward. "We have a warrant to search the house, Miss Eastman. These men — " he motioned to the group behind him "— are looking for a runaway slave."

Laura clutched the sewing in her lap, stabbing her hand on the needle as she did so. The sudden pain made her more annoyed than ever. "Then please proceed," she said. She tried to look composed, though her hands were shaking. "My father won't be happy at the way your men are treating the furniture."

"They aren't my men," the sheriff said unhappily. "They've come in from the South, mostly, and the law says I have to cooperate with them. You know I wouldn't come here on my own. Your father is an old friend of mine and I don't want to lose his good will." He stepped aside and turned to the men in the hallway. "Come in and look around — and be quick about it."

The men shuffled uneasily and murmured among themselves. Two of them took a few steps into the room and glanced about. Walt was the only one who failed to look embarrassed. He strolled to the wardrobe and took a leisurely survey of Laura's dresses, crisply ironed and scented with lavender.

One of the other men said, "Come on, Walt. We don't need to worry about this room. This little southern lady isn't going to harbor any slave in here."

Walt stooped to inspect the floor of the wardrobe and rapped on the wall beside it, as if looking for a hidden room.

Laura bent her head over her sewing to hide her anxious eyes. By the time they finally left, she felt limp.

The group went across the hall to her parents' room, poked their heads into the sewing room, and then clattered down the stairs.

The sheriff came back to Laura to apologize again for the intrusion. "I hope you realize I'm just doing my duty. Tell your pa that, will you?"

"Yes, I'll tell him."

For a moment after the sheriff left, Laura sat without moving. Then she went into the hall, where she could hear the men who were gathered downstairs in the entrance.

"You think he got away?" one asked.

"I figure he wasn't here at all. Maybe Joel never brought him. Or if he did, that little spitfire upstairs wouldn't let him in."

"Did you hear her? 'No *southern* gentleman would think of doing such a thing!' "

This remark was followed by laughter.

Another voice said grimly, "I'm not so sure. Did you see those clothes hanging behind the stove? Bert said they were his, but I don't believe it, not for a minute. I say let's keep an eye on the house."

The sheriff cut in. "Let's go," he ordered.

Laura moaned to herself. How foolish they had been to leave Martin's clothes in plain view. Bert should have known better and so should she.

Feet shuffled in the hall downstairs, and then the door closed.

Bert came up the back way. He was grinning. "Nice job, Sis."

Laura looked up at him, bit her lip, and burst into tears.

Bert said awkwardly, "Hey, don't cry now. It's all over."

Laura rubbed her eyes on her sleeve. "It was terrible! I was so *scared!*"

He looked surprised. "You didn't act scared. You just acted mad." He rolled back the rug. "Let's see how Martin feels." As he lifted the trap door, he announced to Martin, "They've gone."

Martin was obviously shaken. He took a deep breath and raised himself to the edge of the opening. There he slumped down and glanced around the room as if to assure himself that the men were indeed gone.

"I feel like that man in the Bible — Lazarus," he said with a feeble smile. "It's like a tomb in there."

Laura couldn't resist smiling. "Where did you hear about Jesus raising Lazarus from the dead?"

"My pappy used to read the Bible to us every day. All the time he read that book."

"You'd better be thankful for this tomb," Bert told him. "If you'd stayed in the wardrobe in the spare room, you'd be on your way down south right now."

Martin shuddered. "I wasn't easy about that wardrobe. I sure do thank you for taking me out of it. And you, too, Miss Laura, for letting me stay here."

Laura felt that she was receiving credit she didn't deserve. "Bert didn't give me any choice."

"You didn't tell on me," Martin pointed out.

Again she refused to accept his praise. "I had to think of my father. He'd be in bad trouble if you were found here."

Bert looked at her sharply. "Well, whatever your reasons were, I'm glad you kept your mouth shut. We shouldn't have any more trouble now. Joel will come after Martin tonight, and that'll be the end of it."

"Didn't you hear them?" asked Laura. "They saw Martin's clothes in the kitchen, and they said they were going to watch the house!"

Bert groaned. "I knew I should have burned those clothes!"

"They're the only clothes I have!" Martin looked shocked.

"You can keep mine," said Bert. "They're too small for me, anyway."

"Thank you!" Martin smoothed the front of the blue wool shirt. "They're a lot warmer than mine. I need warm clothes here up north."

Laura smiled at him.

"I'll go down and burn those old clothes right now," Martin offered.

"You'd better stay where you are." Bert went to the windows. "If they've got ideas about your clothes, they may come back, thinking they'll catch us by surprise."

Martin looked at Laura. "I don't want to be in Miss Laura's way. Couldn't I go back to the cellar?"

Bert left the window. "Do you know what they did to the sacks of potatoes?"

Martin shook his head, wordless.

"One of those slave hunters took a knife out of his pocket and stabbed it into every bag!"

Laura felt sick. If Martin had been in one of those potato bags, she would never have forgiven herself for keeping him out of the secret room.

"Do I have to stay in the hole?" Martin asked.

"No," Bert replied, "but you have to be able to get into it in a hurry. We'd better figure that out. What if you were all alone here and you heard the slave catchers at the front door?"

"I'd quick jump in the hole and pull the lid on over my head."

"And how would you get the rug back in place?" asked Bert.

Martin thought this over. "I'd reach out of the hole and pull that carpet over the top of me."

Bert looked doubtful. "Let's see you do it."

He and Laura watched while Martin lowered himself into the hidden room and pulled the rug over his head. Like a mole he crawled under it until he had it in place, then wormed back under the carpet to the opening and pulled the trap door shut.

His muffled voice asked, "How's that?"

The rug was wrinkled, but Laura thought Martin had done well under the circumstances.

"You'd better practice," advised Bert, as Martin again came into sight. "Keep working at it until you can do it fast and get the rug smoother." He started for the door. "I'm going down and get rid of your clothes." At the door he paused. "Let's see your shoes."

Martin held up his feet, saying apologetically, "These shoes have done a lot of walking."

Laura could see his feet through the large holes in the bottom of the shoes.

"That's what I thought," Bert said. He trotted down the hall to his room and returned shortly, carrying socks and a pair of shoes. "See if you can wear these."

Martin pulled them on. "Pretty good fit. But they look new. You shouldn't give them to me."

"That's all right," said Bert. "My old shoes would be too small for you. I notice you have good-sized feet for the height of you. Once you get started growing, you'll be a tall fellow."

Laura had recognized Bert's best shoes, but she said nothing. If her brother was willing to wear his everyday shoes to church, that was his affair. But her heart warmed toward him for his generosity.

When Bert left for the kitchen, Laura went down with him. She watched while he stoked the fire in the stove and stuffed in Martin's ragged shirt and trousers. Since they were still damp, they burned slowly. Bert picked up the shoes he had placed on the floor beside the stove and looked despairingly at the smoky fire in the stove. "Guess I'll burn these in the fireplace."

Soon the kitchen, heated by two fires, was uncomfortably warm.

Laura was worried. "Bert, it's too late now, but suppose the slave catchers decide to come back for a closer look at those clothes."

"I'll just say we decided they were too worn-out, not worth keeping after all, so we burned them," Bert said, poking a smoldering shoe.

Laura opened the back door. The bright autumn day seemed to beckon her. The field behind the vegetable garden was aglow with goldenrod and wild asters. Beyond that, the trees in the wood lot were yellow and crimson.

She longed to go outside, but she was afraid of meeting the slave catchers. They might waylay her and ask questions. She especially dreaded meeting the one named Walt. There was something so ruthless about him, she knew he would stop at nothing to get what he wanted. And right now he wanted Martin.

Restlessly she turned back to the kitchen. The clock, ticking loudly on the mantel, caught her eye.

"Eleven o'clock," she said aloud. "Will this day never end?"

Bert added more wood to the stove. "If you'd do a little work, the time would go faster." He picked up a brush and went outside, where he began to clean the potatoes he had dug.

"You don't have to tell me what to do, *little* brother," said Laura. Her pride was injured at criticism from Bert. It used to be the other way around — she was the one who gave him orders.

"Somebody ought to boss you," he called, brushing with furious energy. "You haven't done a lick of work since you came here. In case you've forgotten, up north we don't have slaves to do everything for us."

Laura turned red. She felt like slapping him; she hated to admit that what he said was true.

Laura started up the stairs to her room; then she remembered that it was no longer her refuge, but Martin's. Slowly she returned to the kitchen. She stared at Bert, who was still on the back steps, brushing the potatoes and putting them into a sack. No doubt he'd take them down to the root cellar to store with the other potatoes and the apples and carrots.

Apples, she thought. I'll show *him*.

Snatching up a pan, she hurried to the cellar. She took a dozen apples from a barrel and returned to the kitchen. The fire in the stove was burning well now, and if she was quick about it, she could have fresh applesauce ready for lunch.

Bert grinned wickedly when she called him to lunch. He piled applesauce generously onto one of Mrs. Fitch's biscuits. "What's the idea?" he asked. "Trying to prove you still know how to cook?"

Laura didn't answer, and when he went upstairs with two plates of food for himself and Martin, she told herself she was glad to be alone. Then she heard a burst of laughter from upstairs. It made her feel lonely and left out. She closed and barred the back door, then she, too, filled her plate and climbed the stairs. Bert and Martin were sitting on the edge of the secret opening with their feet dangling in space.

Martin greeted her enthusiastically with, "This is the best applesauce I ever ate."

Bert, too, seemed glad to see her. He slapped the floor beside him. "Have a seat."

"What were you laughing about?" Laura asked, sitting down in the rocker with self-conscious dignity. "I heard you just before I came up."

Bert seemed puzzled and turned questioning eyes to Martin.

Martin looked at Bert and then shyly at Laura. "We were talking about you, Miss Laura, sitting on top of the trap door and those slave catchers saying no little southern lady would hide me! Bert told me how they said that."

Laura was aware that Martin was watching for her reaction, for his big eyes never left her face. She smiled, and he smiled back at her and continued more confidently: "I heard that old chair go creak, creak when you rocked, Miss Laura, and I was ready to bust out laughing down there in that little hole."

"Weren't you scared I'd tell on you?" Laura asked.

Again Martin seemed to hesitate. He glanced at Laura and then fastened his eyes on the floor. Finally he said, almost in a whisper, "I was praying you wouldn't."

So he had been afraid she'd tell on him! Well, she hadn't earned his trust, she admitted. He trusted Bert. Martin talked to him as freely as — as he'd talk to another black boy. But when he spoke to her, he seemed to be afraid of displeasing her. She had noticed the same manner in Uncle Jim's slaves whenever they spoke to white people.

She became aware that Martin was staring earnestly at her, so she said gently, "Go ahead. Don't be afraid to speak up."

"I was just going to say — " Again Martin's gaze traveled to the floor. "Nobody who took me in told on me ever since I ran away. Lots of folks hid me, black folks and white ones. They could've sent me back to my master for the big reward, but they didn't."

"So lots of people helped you," Laura said thoughtfully.

"Yes'm. I couldn't even count how many. Moses, she said people who help the poor runaway slaves are the kindest people in the world."

"Moses?" Bert laughed. "Moses was a *man* and he lived hundreds of years ago."

Martin shook his head. "Not the Moses I mean. She's a woman, all right, and she's as black as I am, and she led a whole lot of slaves to the Promised Land."

"Oh!" Bert looked delighted. "I know who you mean. Her name's Harriet Tubman, isn't it? She was a slave, herself, and she escaped to Canada. Then she went back down south and helped other slaves to get away."

"Miss Tubman, that's her name. Only everybody calls her Moses. My pappy talked to her and he told her how his master was going to sell him down south and split up our family. So when Miss Tubman was ready to go north, she came outside our cabin and sang, "Go Down, Moses." My pappy heard her, and he said, "There's Moses. It's time for us to go.""

"Can you sing it?" asked Bert. "Let's hear that song, 'Go Down, Moses.' "

Martin appeared glad to oblige. He rocked back and forth as he sang softly:

Oh, go down, Moses,
   Way down into Egypt's land,
Tell old Pharaoh,
   Let my people go.

Laura's eyes felt misty. Martin's high, sweet, young boy's voice was appealing. Though she had heard Uncle Jim's slaves sing the same song, she had never guessed its hidden meaning. The slaves must think of themselves as the Israelites, but Pharaoh — who was he? Their master?

"Moses leads the slaves to the Promised Land?" she asked, wondering.

"That's right, Miss Laura. She takes them to Canada. That's the Promised Land where we can be free."

"Why didn't you stay with your family?" Laura asked. "They're in Canada already."

"I got sick with measles, and Pappy didn't want to make trouble for the kind Quaker lady we were staying with. She didn't have room to keep hiding so many of us. Moses said I could come on later when I got well, and the Quaker lady took care of me. Miss Tubman, she — "

Bert raised his hand for silence. "Listen. Someone's at the front door."

A Present for Laura

The bell in the front hall jangled softly.

Laura felt the now-familiar ache of fear return to her chest. Not again! She thought.

At the first sound, Martin had slid into the secret room and was pulling at the rug. Bert said nothing, and his mouth was set in a tight, straight line. He reached for the trap door, but Laura stopped him. She gathered up the dishes from which they had been eating and handed them to Martin. If it were the searchers back at the door, there must be no evidence of lunch for three in her bedroom.

Bert nodded his approval, then set the trap door in place and unrolled the rug before he left to answer the bell.

Laura pulled her rocking chair into the middle of the room and sat in it, tense and quiet, waiting for the thud of boots on the stairs.

Instead, she heard Bert call with a hint of laughter in his voice, "Come down, Laura! Here's a young fellow with a present for you."

Who would send her a present? Joel came to her mind at once, and she ran eagerly down the stairs.

A small boy whom she didn't recognize stood in the hallway, clutching a package wrapped in plain brown paper and tied firmly with string.

As she descended the stairs, he came toward her, asking in a stiff, proper little voice, "Are you Miss Laura Eastman?"

She crouched down to his size. "Yes, I am. And who are you?"

"I'm Harvey, Miss, and this is for you. The boy who — the boy who sent this said to tell you he can't come to see you tonight." Harvey thrust the package into her hands and would have left if she hadn't caught his arm.

Laura was dismayed at the message. She was sure the boy had memorized it. Did this mean Joel couldn't come after Martin tonight?

"You'd better step into the kitchen and have a cookie before you go away," she said.

He considered this solemnly. "Yes, all right."

Bert followed them to the kitchen. "Who sent you, Harvey?"

"I'm not to say." He accepted a cookie from Bert. "Thank you."

Laura turned the package over in her hands. It must be from Joel. She remembered how he had brought her the kitten after their quarrel over the trapped rabbit. Was this a peace offering, too?

"Well, open it!" said Bert.

She wished she could be alone when she opened it. A present was a rare and exciting thing, especially one from Joel. It felt like a book. A book of poems, perhaps? A novel by Charles Dickens? Bert and Harvey were watching her expectantly.

She broke the string and removed the paper. It was a book. She turned it over and read the title — *Uncle Tom's Cabin*.

Laura felt as if she'd been slapped. This was no apology. It was an insult! This was that abolitionist book Joel had said she should read. You couldn't believe those abolitionists. Her aunt and uncle had talked about them. Abolitionists were so set on getting rid of slavery, they'd say anything. Almost in tears, she flung the book onto the table where it landed with a thud.

The little boy jumped and looked dumfounded. Bert picked up the book. "I read this," he said. "It's good."

Harvey licked some crumbs from his hand. "There's a note in the book," he informed Bert. "There." He pulled at a corner of white paper that protruded from between the pages.

Bert pulled out the note and looked inquiringly at Laura.

"Go ahead, read it," she said. Ordinarily she wouldn't have let Bert read a note that was intended for her, but she was so furious at Joel she didn't care what he had written.

Bert unfolded the paper and studied it silently before handing it to his sister. "What do you make of this?"

The short note had no greeting and no signature. It was only four lines long:

Though some may fail,
Those who try on and on will succeed.
Sometimes folly leads to freedom,
And the rabbit escapes from the trap.

While Laura was reading, Harvey started through the pantry, heading for the front door.

Bert strode after him and seized him by both shoulders. "Wait a minute. Who sent the book?"

Harvey said as before, "I'm not to say."

"It's all right to tell us. Whoever sent it would like us to know," Bert urged.

"No." Harvey tried to break free. "I'm not to say!"

"Let him go," Laura said. "I know who sent it." Who but Joel would send her *Uncle Tom's Cabin?* And who else would mention a rabbit in a trap?

She fished another cookie from the tin and gave it to Harvey. "You're a good boy to do as you were told. Go straight home now."

Happy again, Harvey went out of the kitchen and ran down the road. At the first turning, he stopped and waved.

Laura lingered on the steps, glad to let the sun shine on her head. The house was beginning to feel like a prison.

Bert took the note from her fingers. "What's this all about?"

"I have no idea."

"But you said to let Harvey go."

"I know who sent the note — and the book. Joel Todd."

"I guessed that." Bert sat down on the top step. "But Harvey might know something else, such as what this note means."

"I doubt it. Joel must have made the little fellow promise to keep quiet. Harvey was just following orders, and I couldn't see you torturing him to make him break his word."

"I wasn't torturing him!" Bert protested. "You make me sick!"

And you — "

Out of the tail of her eye, Laura saw a little two-wheeled carriage coming down the road from the left. In it was their neighbor, Mrs. Fitch, and it was too late to run into the house. The woman had already seen them.

Bert thrust the note into his pants pocket while Laura sat as if turned to stone. To her amazement and relief, the lady did not get out of the carriage. She merely paused at the end of the path that led from the porch to the road and informed them briskly that she was on her way to town.

"I hear they arrested Richard Todd not an hour ago," she called out. Laura could see she was delighted to have gossip to pass on. "I'm going right over to comfort his poor wife."

"What did Mr. Todd do?" asked Bert.

"I *hear* he had one of those fugitive slaves hid in his house." Mrs. Fitch pulled her shawl more firmly about her narrow shoulders. "People who take the law in their own hands are bound to get into trouble."

"Did they catch the slave?" Bert asked.

"No, I hear he got away." She shuddered. "I only hope I don't meet up with him."

With this remark she gave the reins a slap and continued west on the road to Lewiston.

As soon as Mrs. Fitch was out of sight, Laura and Bert went inside and shut the door.

"So that's why Joel can't come tonight!" Laura exclaimed. "He *said* they had a slave hidden in his house. Imagine Mr. Todd being in jail!" Mrs. Fitch was right, she thought. People who helped the slaves were just asking for trouble.

"I don't see why Joel couldn't come, anyway," mused Bert. "*He's* not in jail."

Laura was positive Joel was not coming. She reminded Bert, "Harvey said very clearly, 'The boy who sent this said he can't come to see you tonight.' You heard him."

"I know." Bert sighed. "Maybe I'd better go talk to Joel."

"And leave me here? What if the slave catchers come back? I'd be scared to death!" She remembered too clearly Walt's rudeness. "I wish Prince were still alive."

Bert frowned. "So do I, but you'll be safe enough. Leave Martin in the secret room and no one will find him."

"If you go, I'm going, too."

"Someone ought to watch the house," he protested.

"We can lock the doors."

Bert gave in. "Oh, all right. Come with me, if you're so scared. While I hitch up Sally, go and tell Martin we're leaving."

Laura clapped her hand to her mouth. "What'll Mrs. Fitch think? She'll be at the Todds' when we get there."

Bert grinned. "We'll tell her we've come to comfort poor Joel."

A Message in Code

The Ridge Road to Lewiston was busy. At the end of their lane, Bert and Laura had to wait for a wagonload of logs to rumble past.

Then, finally on their way, Sally trotted past the team of oxen that pulled the timber, only to be stopped by four hogs, ambling across the road in front of them. Sally fidgeted, for she hated to stop for anything or anybody.

The day was bright and crisp. There had been no rain for a week and dust fanned out from the horse's hoofs with every step. When the stagecoach from Rochester dashed by, it left Bert and Laura choking and half-blinded.

Laura sat up straight on the carriage seat beside Bert. Every time they approached another carriage or a person on foot, she glanced fearfully from beneath her bonnet, afraid of meeting the men who had searched the house that morning. They might stop the carriage and ask more questions.

Bert had the same idea, for he warned, "Remember, we're going to town to shop. What are you going to buy?"

"Molasses," said Laura promptly. "And material for a new dress. Blue silk."

As they rode down Center Street past the village green, Laura saw several men lounging on the benches. Sure that they were slave catchers, she kept her face averted.

"There's Mrs. Fitch!" exclaimed Bert. "Wonder why she's going back so soon."

Laura looked up in time to see their neighbor's carriage flash past, headed toward home. Mrs. Fitch, her hands busy with the reins, gave them a brief nod as she went by.

Bert chuckled. "Maybe Mrs. Todd didn't want to be comforted. I guess she knows what a gossip Mrs. Fitch is."

At Fifth Street, they turned left for a short distance and then turned right onto Cayuga. Laura recognized the Todds' pleasant, rambling house. How many times she had gone there to play! Her own mother had been a close friend of Mrs. Todd, so Laura had gone with her to visit from the time she was a baby.

"We have a welcoming committee," muttered Bert.

Seated on the carriage block in front of the house was Walt. Already he had noticed Laura.

"Don't stop!" whispered Laura urgently.

"I won't!" Bert replied out of the side of his mouth.

But Walt would not be ignored. As they drove by, he leaped to his feet and made a low bow. "Greetings, Miss High and Mighty!" he shouted.

Against her will, Laura looked at him and saw the glint of malice in his dark eyes. He was determined to get even with her for this morning. She told herself she didn't care, but she knew it had been unwise to make him her enemy.

At a steady pace, they rounded the next corner, and Bert looked back. He had a clear view for no other house stood in the way.

"There's Joel at the window," he said.

As Laura turned, Joel waved, but it was not exactly a wave. He was motioning them away. It was perfectly clear that he didn't want them to stop.

"Looks as if Joel is a prisoner in his own house," Bert commented.

"Can they do that?" asked Laura.

"They can watch the house, and if he puts a foot outside, they can follow him every place he goes. He doesn't want us to stop because the slave hunters will be suspicious of everyone who talks to him."

"They already suspect us."

"But if we stopped, they'd be *sure*." Bert pulled gently on the reins, for Center Street lay just ahead. "What'll we do now?"

"We'll shop," Laura decided. "Stop at the store."

When they had purchased the molasses, Bert said, "Now shall we buy your blue silk?"

"That was pretend," Laura answered. "I haven't enough money to buy a length of calico, let alone silk!"

Bert climbed into the carriage and pulled Joel's note from his pocket. "I have a feeling this note is trying to tell us something. He reread the few words, mumbling them to himself. "Maybe it's a code message."

"It's nothing of the kind," said Laura. "He's making fun of me. Sending me *Uncle Tom's Cabin!* He knows what I think of that book!"

"How can you know what you think of it? You never read it."

"I don't need to read it. I've heard enough about it."

Bert said, "I never thought you'd let other

people make up your mind for you. You ought to read it yourself and see what you think." He picked up the reins. "We might as well go home. We can't visit Joel, that's sure."

"Wait." Laura put her hand on his sleeve. "Is there anybody else you know who — who helps fugitives? Anybody who might come after Martin? We *have* to get him out of the house tonight."

"That's right," Bert agreed. "Poor fellow, he'd be so disappointed if we didn't get him to the river by midnight."

"Poor Martin, indeed! It'll be poor *us* if Uncle Daniel sees Martin when he comes tomorrow."

A stranger sauntered past the carriage and looked curiously at the two occupants.

"Drive on now," urged Laura. "People will wonder what we're talking about."

Sally moved briskly into the stream of wagons and carriages going down Center Street toward the river.

Bert nodded toward a small shop on their left. "I hear Mr. Tryon is a stationmaster on the Underground. He has the tailor shop over there."

"Then stop, for pity's sake, and ask him to come for Martin!"

"I might be wrong," Bert said cautiously.

"It's a funny thing you don't even know the other Underground Railroad people in your own town!"

"It's safer not to know too many. I just know the Todds for sure, and also the name of a fellow in Lockport who sends fugitives here — Mr. Lyman Spalding." He pulled to the side of the street. "We'll go talk to Mr. Tryon. I can say we have a friend visiting us who wants to catch a boat, and ask him if he can fix his jacket in a hurry. If he's one of us, he'll know what I mean."

Laura crossed the wide street beside Bert, holding her skirts clear of the dust.

A man sat in the window of the tailor shop, cutting a piece of gray material on a table. Sitting behind him in a straight chair was a dark-bearded man, smoking a cigar.

Bert would have opened the door, but Laura tugged at his sleeve and walked on.

"What's the matter?" asked Bert. "*You* wanted to go there."

"Something's wrong," she said quietly. "That man — the one with the beard — doesn't look as if he belongs in there."

Bert was impatient. "Maybe he's waiting for his pants to be mended."

"I doubt it. Mr. Tryon is just starting on a new suit."

Bert said admiringly, "You have your eyes open, don't you? You'd make a first-class agent in the Underground."

"Don't count on that," Laura replied. "I'm not in this because I want to be."

When they were back in the carriage, Bert said thoughtfully, "Tryon. The tailor's name is Josiah Tryon."

"So?"

He again produced the note. "Listen. 'Though some may fail, Those who *try on* and on will succeed.' Notice that? *Try on* sounds like *Tryon*. Do you suppose Joel was telling us to go to Mr. Tryon?"

Laura sighed. "I never knew you had so much imagination. No, I still say that note was just to tease me."

They were nearing the end of Center Street, where the road sloped to the wharf and the American Hotel. Bert turned to the right onto Fourth Street. "I'm going to drive along the river," he said. "I have an idea, and I want to think."

Laura was in no hurry to return home. Riding behind Sally was far pleasanter than sitting at home, jumping at every sound and waiting for the long day to end.

At the River Road, they turned north, keeping the Niagara on their left. Every now and then Laura could see the blue glint of the water through the trees. Here, though wider than at the foot of the Falls seven miles to the south, the river still ran swiftly between lofty banks on its way to Lake Ontario.

Laura had a sudden inspiration. "Do you think you could get Martin across the Suspension Bridge?"

"With the slave catchers watching every person who goes across!" Bert jeered.

Now they were outside the village of Lewiston and the houses were far apart. There was little traffic. On their left, well back from the road and overlooking the river, Laura noticed a huge stone house topped by a tower.

"My, who owns that?" she asked. "That's new, isn't it?"

Bert glanced at the imposing house with its many chimneys. "Judge Horatio Stow built it not long ago. He was a successful lawyer in Buffalo. Got his start here in town at Mr. Cooke's law office, so when he made enough money, he decided to come back here to live. Pa says the Judge likes it here."

Looking across Judge Stow's well-cleared lawns, Laura could see the river far below, and beyond that the steep cliffs of the Canadian shore, ablaze with autumn foliage.

As soon as they passed Judge Stow's property, Bert slowed Sally to a walk and kept his eyes to the left. Laura guessed that he was watching for something, but she couldn't imagine what, for a dense woodland came down to the edge of the road, blotting out the view of the river and Canada. Tall pines stood elbow to elbow with red and gold maples and russet oaks. And the undergrowth was so dense she could see only a few feet into the wilderness.

When a grass-choked lane came into view, Bert sat up alertly.

Laura wondered at his sudden interest. "Where does that lead?" she asked.

"There's a big house in there on the river bank. It's been empty for years." He reined in the horse. "Mr. Amos Tryon — that's Josiah's brother — built it, but he never lived in it." He looked up and down the road as if he were thinking of turning around, but just then a wagon loaded with barrels of apples approached from the north, so Bert again set Sally into motion.

Laura looked back at the overgrown drive. A memory teased at the edge of her mind — a memory of something that had happened so long ago that it seemed to have been in another life.

"I think I know the house," she said slowly. "The house with the cellars."

"That's it!"

"I was in it once — with Joel and Cousin Tessie. Joel dared us to go there with him." Laura was beginning to recall a certain morning when she had been seven or eight. She and Cousin Tessie, who lived on the River Road not far from where they were now, had been playing at Joel's house, and he had dared them to visit the "haunted house on the river."

"We went in through a broken window," she told Bert. "The rooms were all cobwebby. Joel took us down cellar, but Tessie got scared. I was scared, too," she admitted, "but I pretended I wasn't. Joel said there were four cellars, one under the other, all the way down to the river — and you know how high the river bank is here. He wanted to explore all the cellars, but Tessie wouldn't go, so we gave up and went home. Joel and I got spanked for going off without telling anyone, but Tessie didn't get punished. She was visiting me that day and got away without a spanking because she was company. Joel and I didn't think that was fair."

The wagonload of apples was almost out of sight behind them, on its way to Lewiston.

"Do you know what people call that house?" Bert asked.

Laura shook her head.

"Tryon's Folly!" Bert chuckled. "After Amos Tryon spent all that money on the house, his wife wouldn't live in it. People say that's the only mistake he ever made in a money way."

Laura suddenly had an idea. "There was something in Joel's note about folly," she said. "Let me see it." She held out her hand. "After all, it *is* my letter."

Bert handed it to her and she read it aloud:

Though some may fail,
Those who try on and on will succeed.
Sometimes folly leads to freedom,
And the rabbit escapes from the trap.

"That's it, Bert!" she exclaimed with a quickening of interest. " 'Sometimes folly leads to freedom,' might mean that Tryon's Folly leads to freedom for the runaways. Maybe the slaves hide in the cellars until a boat can pick them up and take them across to Canada."

"Eureka, Sis! I think you're right!" Bert beamed at her.

Laura reread the last line. "I suppose the rabbit is Martin."

Now the wagon of apples was out of sight. Again Bert reined in.

"What are you doing?" asked Laura, suddenly alarmed.

"I'm going back and visit Tryon's Folly," he said.

"No, you're not!" She snatched the reins from his hands and set Sally again on the road north.

"I am," he said, though he made no effort to reclaim the reins. "If that old house is the last stop on the Underground Railroad, I've got to go look at it!"

"Bert Eastman! Are you thinking of taking Martin there tonight?"

"Yes. I'm sure you're right — that's where Pa and the Todds take the runaway slaves."

Laura felt angry and helpless. "I won't let you!" She urged Sally to a trot. "It's too dangerous! They'll catch you, and then Pa will be arrested and he'll have to pay a big fine — "

"They won't catch me." He put his hands on the reins in front of hers and pulled Sally to a halt.

"I'll get out!" Laura threatened.

"Get out, then."

98

Laura glared at him. "I'll go to the sheriff!"

Bert gazed at her scornfully. "And how would that help Pa?"

A clatter sounded on the road behind them. Laura looked over her shoulder and saw a man, riding a large piebald horse, coming after them full tilt.

Bert sighed and again moved Sally ahead.

Quickly the horse came abreast of their carriage, and a moment later the rider swerved directly in front of them and halted. Sally was so frightened that she reared up on her hind legs.

As the rider leaped down from his horse, Laura recognized the insolent young slave catcher named Walt.

The House with Four Cellars

Walt sauntered back to the Eastman carriage.

"What a picture!" he said. "Brother and sister out for a ride." Though he smiled, his eyes were watchful, and he craned his neck to look into the carriage. "Wouldn't have a third passenger hidden away, would you?"

Laura hoped Bert would give an answer, but he was at Sally's head, giving all his attention to reassuring her.

"What do you mean frightening our horse like that?" demanded Laura hotly.

Walt's hawklike face took on a hurt expression. "Here I was riding peacefully down the road and your horse almost ran me down."

Laura gasped at this outright lie, but Bert said quietly, "No need to argue, Laura. No one's hurt."

"That's right," Walt agreed. "Why can't you be sensible like your brother?" He turned to Bert. "I don't suppose you'd mind if I have a look at your carriage?"

"Can't say I'd like it," Bert said, giving Sally a final pat and strolling back toward Walt. "But I won't stop you."

At this, Walt climbed into the carriage. Immediately Laura scrambled to the ground, and while he examined every inch of the carriage, she stood tensely at Sally's nose, feeding her sprigs of grass.

Walt seemed especially interested in the carriage seat, for he prodded and pushed it and tried to lift it up. The seat, however, didn't stir.

"Where are you headed, Eastman?" he asked.

Laura didn't give Bert a chance to answer, for she was ready for this question. "It's not your business, but I'll tell you anyway. We're on our way to see our Cousin Tessie, down the road a piece."

A look of surprise flashed across Bert's face, but he recovered quickly. "We'd better be moving on," he said. "She'll think we're not coming."

Walt looked from one to the other. "You're not fooling me. I know you're up to something, and I'm watching you until I find out what it is. If you're hiding a slave, I'll see to it you're brought to justice — even if it takes all winter!"

Laura kept her eyes on the horse. Walt had the law on his side. Yet, knowing his spiteful ways, she felt sorry for the unfortunate slave he might track down. No matter what the law said, it couldn't be right to turn a boy like Martin over to such a man.

Walt's face was dark with anger as he turned his black-and-white horse around in the road and sped back toward Lewiston.

Laura returned to her place in the carriage.

"Keep going to Cousin Tessie's," she said abruptly. "Let's make my little lie come true."

Bert protested, "But I want to go to Tryon's Folly! I have to find out if it's a likely place to take Martin tonight."

Laura glanced up at him impatiently. "I want to go there, too."

"You do!"

"Yes, but Walt might come back to see if we're really going to Cousin Tessie's so we'd better go there and *then* to Tryon's Folly."

Bert looked down at her hands clenched tightly in her lap. "Walt got your dander up, didn't he?"

Laura nodded. "He makes me want to fight."

"Good." Bert lifted the reins. "Giddap, Sally!"

Laura tried to recall what it had been like in the cellar at the Tryon house. "We'll need a lantern. I remember it was dark in that cellar, even in the daytime," she said.

Bert chuckled. "You *have* changed!"

Laura squirmed uncomfortably. "I don't know if I've changed. I'm no abolitionist, but I don't want Walt to get Martin."

"I'm glad of that. And you're right about the light. We have a lantern. Pa always carries one on the back of the carriage, but I don't have any way to light it."

"We'll ask Cousin Tessie if we can borrow a few lucifers. We won't have to explain why we want them. Or do we dare tell her about Martin?"

Bert shook his head. "No. I imagine she thinks the way Pa and I do, but I'm not sure. It's best not to get her mixed up in this."

Laura patted the cushion on which they sat. "Why was Walt so interested in this?"

A faint smile lifted the corners of Bert's wide mouth. "Some people have a hidden compartment under their carriage seats."

"Do we have one?"

"Not in this carriage, but there's one in the wagon Pa and Abby took to Buffalo. I wish we had the wagon now. It'd make it easier to get Martin through town tonight." He drove in silence a minute and then he said, "Maybe it's a good thing Walt stopped us. He won't be so suspicious if he sees me driving out this way tonight. He'll figure I'm just going to Cousin Tessie's again."

"Where'll you hide Martin?"

"On the floor, I guess. I'll put the lap robe over my knees and he can lie under it."

They made their visit with Cousin Tessie brief. In answer to her pleas that they stay for supper, they gave the excuse of chores to be done at home.

As they once again reached the woods around Tryon's Folly, Bert gazed cautiously up and down the River Road. Then he turned Sally onto the rough drive that led to Tryon's Folly. Laura did not breathe easily until trees hid them from the road. She could not bear to think of what would happen if Walt should see them riding up this abandoned lane.

When they were several yards into the woods, Bert jumped down and broke off a leafy branch which he used to brush out the marks left behind them by the carriage wheels and the horse's hoofs.

"Don't want anyone to notice that a rig turned in here," he explained.

The lane grew fainter as they progressed. Bushes crowded close on either side, and the road itself was pitted with holes. Laura clung to the carriage lest she be bounced over the side. Finally Sally came to a complete halt at a tree that had fallen across the road.

"We go the rest of the way on foot," said Bert. He stared ahead. "Looks rough. Want to wait here?"

Laura climbed down. "No, I want to see the place again, myself. I was here so long ago. I can't remember much about it."

Bert took the lantern from the rear of the carriage and went ahead. Laura followed closely, picking her way carefully in her thin shoes and holding up her long skirts so they wouldn't catch on branches and underbrush.

When they emerged from the cover of the trees, the first view of the house took her breath away. She had forgotten how large and impressive it was. Covered with gray stucco, it was a long, rectangular building, two stories high. Two chimneys rose above the peaked roof, one near the center of the house and the other at the south end.

"What a pity Mrs. Tryon never lived in it!" Laura exclaimed softly. Then, with her eyes on the wall of trees, she added, "It *would* be lonely. I can see why she didn't want to stay here."

"A person could cut down some of the trees," said Bert. "If it were mine, I'd make a clearing around the house and have a big lawn. Then I'd trim enough trees on the river bank so there'd be a view of the water. I always wanted to live by the river," he confided.

"You did? So did I." Laura's eyes met Bert's in a brief moment of complete agreement. She realized they had been speaking quietly, though there was little chance that anyone would overhear them. The house was far from the River Road and had no near neighbors.

In spite of the fact that the walls of the house were solid and undamaged, the place had the look of a ruin because of the many windows that were broken. They'd have no trouble getting inside, Laura thought, though they might be cut by slivers of glass.

Bert, however, took the direct approach. He walked boldly up the steps to the front door and turned the knob. With a slight creaking, the door opened, and he and Laura stepped inside.

They found themselves in a large room. At their entrance a bird flew out of a window, startling them. Feathers and bird droppings littered the floor of the room, and cobwebs laced the corners. Several dark objects the size of mice clung to the upper walls and ceiling. After staring at them for several moments, Laura realized with a shudder that they were bats. She hoped they would stay where they were.

"I don't feel right, walking in like this." Her voice echoed in the unfurnished room.

"Joel practically sent us here," said Bert.

"Yes, I'm sure he meant for us to come," Laura agreed, "and it isn't as if we were going to hurt the house." She tried to feel reassured about their trespassing. After all, no one had ever lived here.

Bert interrupted her thoughts. "Where's the cellar? Do you remember?"

Laura examined the long room where they stood, noting the huge stone fireplace and the row of windows facing the river.

"This is the parlor, I suppose, and next to it is the dining room, and then the kitchen." She picked her way across a slippery patch of broken glass to the sunny kitchen, where the fireplace stood ready for use with pot hooks in place. Yet, no one had ever cooked a meal in it.

"I think this goes to the cellar." Laura opened a door on her left. Stairs descended into darkness.

Bert set the lantern on the kitchen floor and knelt to light it. He started cautiously down the steps, holding the lantern before him at arm's length. Laura, following him, knew they couldn't have seen much without the lantern, for the small windows of the cellar were dirty and covered with cobwebs, admitting only a faint light.

Bert crouched to examine the floor. "Looks as if people have walked through here, don't you think so?"

"I don't know, and let's not waste our time playing detective." Laura circled slowly. "We need to find out how to get to the next cellar." A door set in the west wall caught her eye. "That must be it. At least it's on the side toward the river." She crossed to the door and pulled it open. Bert came forward with the lantern, illuminating a tunnel that sloped downward.

From then on the way was clear, for one cellar led to another like steps descending the river bank. Laura followed Bert and the dim glow of the lantern through the tunnel, down a short flight of stairs to a second cellar, through a trap door, and down more stairs to the third cellar. Finally a narrow ladder brought them to the fourth cellar, where a spring filled a shallow basin and overflowed into a drain in the stone floor. In this last cellar they found a heavy plank door. This surely must lead to the river bank.

Bert pushed the door open, and he and Laura saw before them a wall of bushes. At their feet a path wound steeply down toward the river, still far below. Again they shared a look of agreement.

Laura said, "This *has* to be the place where Joel intended to take Martin tonight."

A Fugitive Is Captured

Bert ventured a few feet down the path, but then raced back to Laura and pulled her into the cellar.

"There's someone out there in a boat," he cautioned.

"They can't see us with all those bushes," Laura pointed out.

"I suppose you're right," Bert conceded. "But I'll be in trouble with Pa and Joel if the slave catchers find out about this place because of me. Pa never told me where he took the runaways. Guess he didn't think I could keep still about it."

"*I* think Pa wanted to keep you safe. It's dangerous business, you know. Anyway," she consoled him, "Joel must have trusted you or he wouldn't have sent that note."

Bert's face brightened, but he said only, "He was desperate."

Laura crossed the narrow cellar, crouched beside the pool, and scooped up a handful of water. It was clear and cold. She tasted it and found it good. "A slave could stay here a long time," she remarked. "Do you suppose Amos Tryon built these cellars on purpose to hide the fugitives?"

Bert shook the ladder, testing its strength. "Course not. Probably he planned to use this cellar for his springhouse. Butter and milk would keep well in that cold water."

Laura began to see the possibilities of the river-bank cellars. "One could be a laundry room. They could pipe the water up from this spring. And another could be a wine cellar." She gazed around the small room where they stood. "I guess if these cellars had been planned for the slaves, there'd be some secret hiding places down here. I don't see any place where a slave could get out of sight if the slave catchers came around."

Bert agreed. "It was too easy for us to find our way through the cellars." He sighed. "I guess no place is perfect. At least this is hidden from the road, and it's on the river."

Laura stepped outside again and gazed up at the steep banks on either side of the house. "The cellars certainly are the best way to reach the river. A person could climb down the bank, but it would be dangerous."

Bert started up the ladder. "Let's go home. Martin will be worried."

When they emerged from the house, the sun was still bright, though it was low in the sky. Bert paused only to blow out the lantern before they took the path through the woods.

"I wish you didn't have to come back to-night," Laura worried. "I know I'd hate to come through here in the dark."

"Maybe Joel will come, and I won't have to take Martin."

"You'd be disappointed if you couldn't go," she challenged him.

"Maybe I would at that."

"I think you and Joel and Pa aren't in this Underground Railroad just because of the slaves. It's an adventure."

Bert glanced back at her over his shoulder. "You wouldn't understand. Pa says a man's conscience is stronger than the law. And he says laws can be bad. Like the Fugitive Slave Law. Do you know that law says a slave catcher can swear any black he finds is the fugitive he's looking for, and the black hasn't any right to speak for himself?" He pushed on down the lane, muttering, "That old Henry Clay; he's to blame for getting the law passed."

Laura thought of pointing out that Henry

Clay wasn't the only person to blame, but rather than get into an argument, she changed the subject. "I suppose Martin couldn't find this place alone?"

"Of course he couldn't. In the dark? And it wouldn't be safe for him to be wandering around. The minute anyone saw him, they'd know who he was."

Sally whinnied her pleasure at seeing Laura and Bert again.

Laura ran ahead to see if anyone was on the road, while Bert backed the carriage down the narrow lane. The leaves rustled under her feet, making, she felt, too much noise. And what would anyone think, seeing her burst forth from the woods with her hair flying and her bonnet hanging down her back? Slowing her pace, she slipped into the denser shadow of a pine tree. Here she stood motionless, listening for the sound of hoofs or wagon wheels on the River Road. All she heard was the creak and rustle of their own carriage on the lane and Sally's snort of protest at being forced to back so far.

Encouraged, she peered around the tree and finally emerged boldly onto the edge of the road. No one was in sight.

She ran back to Bert. "Hurry! The road's clear!"

Remembering how he had removed their tracks on the way to Tryon's Folly, she snatched up a branch, and as soon as the carriage was again on the road, she whisked out the tracks at the entrance to the lane.

"Jump in!" Bert urged. "No telling when someone will come along."

They had been under way only a minute or two and were approaching Judge Stow's house when a horse and rider pounded toward them.

"That was close," murmured Bert.

The rider slowed his horse and shouted to them, "They caught a slave in Lewiston! I'm rounding up help to set him free!"

"Good!" shouted Bert.

When the rider had gone on, Laura asked fearfully, "Do you think it's Martin?"

Bert slapped the reins. "Giddap!" he shouted. "How do I know? He should have been safe enough, provided he stayed where we left him."

"We've been gone a long time. Maybe he decided we'd deserted him. Or maybe the slave catchers broke into the house and found him."

Bert agreed with maddening calm. "It may be," was all he said.

Laura stared anxiously ahead. Perhaps at

this very moment Walt was taking Martin back to the master who had beaten him. "Can't that horse go any faster?"

"Of course she can. She's the fastest horse for miles around. But if we go racing down the road, someone's going to wonder why we're in such a hurry and maybe follow us home."

"Oh, all right!" Laura sat back on the seat and yanked her bonnet into place on her head. "Are you going to try to set the runaway free, whoever he is?" She was so sure Bert would say yes, she wondered why she even asked, but to her amazement he shook his head.

"Pa says we shouldn't draw notice to ourselves. We can do more good working in secret."

On Center Street, the press of people became thick in spite of the wideness of the road. Bert jumped down from the carriage, and flinging the reins to Laura, called out, "Wait here!"

From her vantage point on the carriage seat, Laura could see her brother pushing his way through the crowd that poured up the street to the east.

Laura called out to a woman passerby, "Where's everyone going?"

"To the Presbyterian church. They cornered a runaway slave there!"

The church was on Cayuga Street, not far from Joel's house.

Laura pulled Sally to the side of the road in front of Mr. Josiah Tryon's tailor shop. Through the window she could see Mr. Tryon, working as if nothing were going on outside. The dark-bearded man who had been with him before was still there, standing near the window.

If Mr. Tryon was a leader of the Underground Railroad, would he sit inside there with his back to the window? Yes, maybe he would. Just as Bert said, he wouldn't want to be noticed as a sympathizer.

Near the tailor shop, a narrow road called Niagara Street led south toward Cayuga. It was a small street, little more than an alleyway. The crowd was ignoring this short cut. Only a few people broke away from the rest and ran down it.

Laura hesitated only a moment. Bert had said to wait, but she had just as much right as he to find out if the captured fugitive was Martin.

She stepped down from the carriage and tied Sally to the hitching post. Then, with her skirt lifted above her ankles, she fled down Niagara Street. She ran until she was out of breath. Then she walked as rapidly as she could past Plain Street and on toward Cayuga. When she slowed down to catch her breath, she caught snatches of conversation from the others who hurried toward the church.

"We ought to lynch them. Show those southerners we know how to do it, too."

Laura looked in amazement at the speaker, a gentle-faced man with white hair hanging over his ears in a fringe.

"Those slave catchers have no business coming up north," the white-haired man declared. "Ought to give them a taste of their own medicine."

Hearing this, Laura realized he was in favor of lynching the slave catchers, not the captured slave. She set her lips firmly together. What should a person think in these days? One thing she was sure of — lynching was wrong, no matter who the victim was.

The Fastest Horse in Town

At Cayuga Street, Laura turned left and passed directly in front of the Todd house. Men were still posted there, near the front and rear entrances.

Joel had the window to the right of the porch wide open and was leaning out so far that he was in danger of falling into the bed of zinnias below. His hair was tousled by the wind and his eyes were snapping with excitement. Although Laura was only a few feet from him, he seemed to pay no attention to her. His eyes were on the crowd up the street.

Thus ignored, Laura hurried by with burning cheeks. She wished she knew why he had failed to greet her. Was it because he didn't want the guard at the front door to know they were acquainted? Or couldn't he forgive her for her southern sympathies? Perhaps, she thought sadly, they would never again be friends.

Across the street, on the southeast corner of Cauyga and Fifth streets, stood the Presbyterian church. It was built of stone and was quite imposing with its bell tower and its front portico with four graceful columns. The two large front doors at either end of the porch were closed, and several men stood before them, holding off the crowd that filled the lawn and overflowed onto the road in front of the building.

"Set him free!" shouted a man. At once the call was repeated by many voices. "Set him free!"

Again Laura was torn by conflicting emotions. All these people were concerned over one black man. They had stopped whatever they were doing to come to look at him and to try to keep him from being sent back down south.

Yesterday she couldn't have understood this, but now she knew Martin — and that made all the difference in the world. Before, she had thought of slaves as property belonging to plantation owners such as Uncle Jim. But now, because of Martin, she knew that slaves were *people*. And it was only right that a person should have the chance to live a life of his own. No one should own a *person*.

At the right side of the church, two boys were taking turns boosting each other up so they could see into a small window that was an inch or two ajar. As she watched, she saw an angry sheriff's deputy chase them away. Laughing, the boys ran down the slope.

Laura scurried after them and, panting, asked, "Did you see him?"

"Who?" asked the elder of the two boys.

"The runaway."

"I just saw him a minute."

"What does he look like?"

"Black," said the boy. He exchanged a glance with his friend and laughed. "He looks like any black man. They all look alike."

Laura felt indignant. The very idea — saying all blacks looked alike! You might as well say all white people looked alike. They were thin or fat or old, or they were young like Martin and had big eyes that could look scared or merry or grateful —

Something was happening on the porch of the church. Shouts and a sound of scuffling reached her ears, but from where she stood, she couldn't see what was going on. The few people who were not already crowded

120

around the front porch of the church hurried to get there.

Laura was about to go up the hill again when she noticed a man wearing a deputy's badge slip quietly into a small side door near the rear of the church. Less than a minute later he came out leading a tall, slim black dressed in a shabby blue shirt and tan pants. Behind him was another deputy.

At the same moment, a carriage came hurtling down Fifth Street from the direction of town. One glance told Laura that it was the Eastman carriage drawn by Sally, galloping for all she was worth. Down the hill she came, directly toward Laura, who stood speechless and motionless. Someone pushed her roughly back against the wall of the church. Afterward she couldn't say whether it was one of the deputies or the black who had shoved her to safety. But confused though she was, she looked hard at the two men in the carriage. One she had never seen before, but the other was the black-bearded man who had been in Josiah Tryon's tailor shop.

The black-bearded man who had the reins shouted to Sally and pulled her to a halt. He reached out of the carriage, seized the black by the wrist, and hoisted him into the carriage beside him. With a crack of the whip, the carriage was off again, continuing down the hill — even faster than before.

Someone in the crowd in front of the church shouted, "There he goes!" Two men, both of whom Laura recognized as being among the slave hunters who had come to the house looking for Martin, leaped into a carriage and took chase.

Laura doubted that they could catch up, for the first carriage had a long head start, and Sally, as Bert had said, was the fastest horse in town.

One of the deputies, who had been with the black, disappeared into the church, but a crowd quickly gathered around the other deputy. Laura, with her back against the rough stone wall of the church, found that she couldn't leave unless she were to push her way through the horde of men. Timidly she remained where she was, getting more and more uncomfortable and uneasy.

"What happened? Why'd you let him go?" a man asked the deputy.

The deputy seemed as puzzled as Laura.

"We were going to move him over to the sheriff's house for safekeeping. You never can tell what might happen with a crowd like this, and we didn't want anybody getting hurt. Next thing we knew that carriage came down the hill, and a fellow grabbed the fugitive and took off with him."

"You should have had him handcuffed to you. Sounds to me like you didn't put up much of a fight."

To Laura's dismay, the slave hunter named Walt joined the group. "We're going to get to the bottom of this!" he declared. "I think you had this all set up!"

"We were going to take him to the courthouse in Lockport as soon as we could," protested the deputy. "We want justice done, same as you."

"I don't like your idea of justice!" Walt snarled. As the deputy started to walk away, Walt reached out to seize him, but several of the local citizens came quietly between the two men, giving the deputy time to escape.

Laura, seeing an opening, edged away from the wall of the church and started up the hill. She had taken only a few steps when Walt blocked her way.

"Miss Eastman! What do you know about this?" he demanded. "You were down here when it happened. I saw you."

"N-nothing," she stammered.

"That was your horse and carriage. I'd

know it anywhere. Who was in that carriage?" he insisted.

"I don't know!" She tried to get around him, but as quickly as a cat he leaped in front of her again.

Walt glared at her. "You're no southerner! You're just like everyone else in this town — ready to break the law."

"Let me go!" Laura cried out.

"I'm not through with you yet!"

Laura was close to despair. The crowd was scattering and no one seemed to pay any attention to her. Then she saw Bert coming toward them. He had never looked as good to her as he did at that moment. She ducked wildly around Walt and ran to her brother.

Bert growled, "You leave my sister alone," and to Laura's surprise, Walt backed away. It couldn't be that he was afraid of a tall, thin, thirteen-year-old! It must be that he had seen the sheriff coming down the church steps and realized he would get no sympathy from that source.

Bert took Laura's elbow and said quietly, "Let's go."

"That was our carriage," she whispered, still trembling.

"I know it." Bert sounded impatient. "And so does everyone else. Everyone in town knows Sally. Wait till Pa hears about this. We'll really be in trouble." He looked accusingly at Laura. "Why didn't you stay in the carriage?"

"I wanted to see if it was Martin. I had just as much right to look as you did."

Bert dropped the subject. "I wish I knew who was in that carriage."

"One of the men was that fellow we saw in Mr. Tryon's shop today. The man with the black beard."

"Is that so? Well!" Bert looked hopeful. "I wonder . . ."

"What do you wonder?"

Bert glanced around to see if anyone was near them. "That man might be connected with the Underground Railroad."

"Of course it was someone from the Underground," Laura said positively. "Who else would steal a fugitive away?"

"Some of the slave catchers might. It's the fellow who takes a slave down south who gets the bounty."

A carriage drawn by a sturdy black horse came up beside them. The sheriff leaned out. "Do you and your sister need a ride home, Bert?"

"Thanks. We sure do."

As they traveled out the Ridge Road

toward home, Laura couldn't help smiling to herself as she tried to guess what Mrs. Fitch would think if she saw them being taken home by the sheriff.

When he stopped in front of the Eastman house, the sheriff said, "Don't worry about your horse and carriage. I'm sure we'll get them back for you."

Laura wondered how he could be so positive.

The Rights of a Human

The house had a deserted look. No one would guess a runaway slave was hiding inside, Laura reflected, as the sheriff dropped them off at the end of the drive.

As soon as they had closed the door behind them, Bert called out, "Martin! We're back! It's Bert and Laura!"

There was no answer. At once the thought flashed through Laura's mind: he's gone! The slave catchers came while we were away and found him.

Bert took the stairs two at a time, shouting, "Martin! You hear me?"

Laura lifted her long skirts and hurried after him. As she approached her room, she heard Martin's now-familiar voice, slightly muffled, "I'm here, Mr. Bert. Soon's I heard someone come on the porch, I ducked down into the little hole. I thought it was you, but I didn't dare take a chance."

When Laura reached her room, Martin had pushed aside the carpet and was crawling out of the secret room.

"I'm glad to see you!" she exclaimed. "They caught a runaway in the church and for a while we were afraid it was you."

Martin's eyes widened.

"He got away," Laura assured him. "I think he must have been George — the slave who was hiding at Joel's house."

"Did anyone come here?" asked Bert.

"Nope. But every time I heard a noise, I jumped back in this hole." Martin turned to Bert. "Where's your carriage? I didn't hear it come in."

Bert explained how their carriage had been taken. "So now we have to figure out another way to get you to the river tonight."

In the excitement, Laura hadn't thought of this. "Bert! You can't take him through town on foot."

"We'll go through the woods."

Laura said firmly, "You'd never be able to find your way at night. You'll just have to wait till Pa gets home."

Bert set his jaw stubbornly. "Don't try to tell me what I can do. A boat's coming to pick

Martin up at midnight, and I'm going to have him there to meet it. If we don't get there tonight, the plans have to be made all over again. How long do you think we can keep him hidden? Uncle Daniel will be here by morning."

Laura recognized her mistake. It was no use telling Bert what to do. "All right," she said. "You figure it out."

"Where are you going to take me?" Martin asked nervously.

Laura said, "You tell him about Tryon's Folly, Bert. I'm going down and get some supper for us."

By six-thirty supper was finished and the dishes were washed. The evening stretched ahead endlessly.

Laura accompanied Bert when he went out to feed the chickens. She stared anxiously at the sky, hoping to find clouds that would provide an early cover of darkness, but the entire sky was clear. The quarter moon looked ready and able to light up the land for hours.

Bert noticed his sister looking at the sky. "Don't get your hopes up," he said. "The moon doesn't set until ten-thirty tonight. I looked in the almanac to be sure. I don't dare take Martin out until after it goes down. Even if it isn't a full moon, it gives more light than I want tonight."

All three gathered in Laura's room to be near Martin's hiding place. Bert closed the inside shutters so any watchful eyes would be unable to see three figures walking about where there should have been only two.

Martin seated himself on the floor beside the lamp table to read a well-worn paper Bert had given him. Laura noticed the masthead, *Frederick Douglass' Paper*.

"What's that?" she asked.

"It's an abolitionist paper," Bert answered. "You know, against slavery. It used to be called *The North Star*, because slaves follow the North Star to freedom. It's put out by a man who used to be a slave, Frederick Douglass."

Laura stared at him. "You mean the editor is a *black* man?"

Bert smiled. "He is, and what's more, I've seen him."

Martin looked up with an awed expression. "You've *seen* Mr. Douglass?"

"I stood as close to him as I am to you right now. He came to Lockport to give a talk. He's handsome — big, with a head of hair like a lion."

Laura was stunned. In the south, even the suggestion that a black man could write and run a newspaper would be unthinkable.

"Let me see that for a second, Martin." Bert held out his hand for the paper. He studied it until he found what he wanted. "Here it is. Pa showed this to me. He says that in a few words this tells the whole story of what he believes in. Listen." Bert read aloud. " 'I know of no rights of race superior to the rights of humanity.' "

"Did Frederick Douglass write that?" Laura asked.

Bert nodded.

Laura thought a moment. "It's true, isn't it?" she exclaimed. "A person should have the rights of a human being, no matter what color he is. That's the meaning, isn't it?"

"I think so," said Bert. "Or maybe that being white doesn't give us the right to take away a black person's human rights."

"Only, what are the rights of a human being?" Laura asked thoughtfully.

"To be free," said Martin.

"And to be treated with respect," Laura added.

Bert suggested, "Life, liberty, and the pursuit of happiness, as the Declaration of Independence says."

Have I been asleep for four years? Laura wondered. She asked herself why she hadn't thought about such things before. Uncle Jim and Aunt Ruth and their friends seemed to think it was natural and right that blacks should be slaves. And she had accepted their attitude without questioning it!

The clock on the stairs boomed seven times. More than three hours before Bert and Martin could leave.

"Maybe you two should get some rest," Laura suggested. "I'll stay on watch."

"I couldn't sleep," said Bert. "How about you, Martin?"

"I won't sleep again till I'm across the river." He grinned. "I'll sleep in the Promised Land."

Bert paced back and forth. "I'll be glad when you're there." He went to the front window, lifted a slat in one of the shutters, and peered out. "I wonder if Joel will be able to get away."

"If he thought he could come, he wouldn't have sent that note," Laura snapped. "Stop pacing around. Can't you find something to do?"

Bert stared at her. "What's the matter? You don't have anything to worry about. I'm the one who has to get Martin to the river."

A mischievous gleam came into his eyes and he bolted from the room. When he came back, he had a book in his hand. "Martin and I can keep busy. We'll take turns reading out loud."

Martin looked pleased. "I'd like that."

Bert sat down on the floor near Martin and opened the book. "*Uncle Tom's Cabin,*" he read, "by Harriet Beecher Stowe."

Laura felt angry and hurt. She had changed many of her ideas that day, but she still wasn't ready to accept *Uncle Tom's Cabin.* Uncle Jim had said it was a pack of lies. "I told you I didn't want to see that book!" she exclaimed.

"Don't look, then." Bert held the book higher to catch the light on the page.

Martin was lying on his back, a rapt expression on his face. "I always did want to read *Uncle Tom's Cabin.*"

Laura went into the hall. She'd go down to the kitchen and sit. She could find something to read, too. Behind her Bert's voice went on with the reading. She looked back at the room where the lamp spread a pool of light on the carpet. It was in marked contrast to the dark hall. There was companionship, at least, in that room. She sighed and went back. Taking up her sewing, she sat down in her rocker.

Bert said teasingly, "Thought you were going to leave us."

Laura wrinkled her nose at him. "I might as well hear the foolish thing."

When Bert tired of reading, Martin took over. Despite herself, Laura became so lost in the story that she forgot to move her needle. Can it be true slaves are treated like that? she asked herself. Then she remembered Martin's scars, and things she hadn't paid attention to when she was living with her aunt and uncle — frightened black faces, hurried whispers.

Now Martin had reached the part where Uncle Tom was sold down south. "That almost happened to my pappy!" he exclaimed. "Master was going to sell him and we'd never see him again. Only my pappy isn't like Uncle Tom. He wouldn't let our family be split, so we all ran away!"

So it *did* happen like that. When she thought about it, Laura remembered how the owner of a plantation near Uncle Jim's had sold a man and woman down south. He kept their children and had one of the other slaves take them in.

Martin was an uneven reader. Often he

had to stop to ask Bert how to pronounce a word. Laura finally became impatient. "Here, let me read for a while," she said. She pulled her chair close to the lamp table.

The clock chimed and Laura stopped reading to count the strokes. Nine o'clock! She was amazed. The time was going much faster — almost too fast.

She read on.

Fifteen or twenty minutes later, Martin jumped up from the floor and whispered excitedly, "Somebody's coming!"

Laura closed the book, keeping the place with her finger. In the silence she heard voices outside. Footfalls sounded on the front steps. She knew at once it wasn't Pa and Abby and Uncle Daniel. It was too soon for them, and besides, they would come to the back door. Laura felt her heart leap with fear. Who could be coming at this hour of the night?

Bert Is Arrested

The bell sounded through the entire house. Martin covered his ears as if he couldn't endure the clamor.

Bert said defiantly, "We'll not go to the door!"

Motionless, the three sat in silence. On and on the ringing continued until Laura thought the bell pull must break. Would their unwanted visitor never go away?

Moving cautiously, Bert rolled back the carpet and motioned Martin into the hole in the floor. Laura found she was still clutching *Uncle Tom's Cabin*. If the slave catchers saw it, they'd be even more sure that a runaway was hidden in the house. Hastily she handed it to Martin before Bert slid the trap door into place.

A shout came from the front steps. "We know you're in there! Open the door!"

"You'll have to let them in," Laura whispered to Bert.

"I'll count ten!" came the deep voice from the porch. "If you aren't here, we'll break in!"

"Hurry!" urged Laura.

Bert was tugging at the carpet. "Wait till I get this straight."

Laura jumped up and helped him, then recovered her sewing and sat tensely waiting.

Bert left the room but returned immediately, saying, "I'll have to take the lamp so I can see who's there."

"All right." Laura dropped her sewing. "I'm coming with you."

They descended the stairs with Bert ahead carrying the lamp. With every step, the counting on the porch came more clearly to their ears. "Six — seven — "

"We're coming!" shouted Bert. "Who's there?"

The counting stopped. "Deputy Smith!" came the answer. "Open up, Bert! I have a warrant for your arrest."

"I haven't done anything wrong!"

"You can explain that. You're wanted for questioning."

Laura heard another voice, one that was painfully familiar. "Don't argue with him. Out of my way and I'll push in the door."

The voice belonged to Walt. She might have known he'd be behind this.

Bert unlocked the door and flung it open.

"What's the idea —?" he began, but at once the two men pushed into the hallway.

Deputy Smith was apologetic. "We saw your carriage pick up the slave this afternoon. Walt, here, convinced the judge you ought to be questioned." He showed Bert the warrant.

"I had nothing to do with that," Bert said. "I left the carriage on Center Street and someone helped himself to it."

"You'll have to come along, anyway," the deputy insisted.

"Tomorrow will be time enough, won't it?" asked Bert. "I don't want to leave my sister here alone."

"She's big enough to look after herself," Walt interrupted.

Deputy Smith looked at Laura, who stood in the shadows behind Bert. "You'll be safe enough, Miss Eastman. No one will bother you. I'll guarantee that. I'm sorry, Bert, you'll have to come with us." He seemed to find his duty unpleasant.

Bert was silent, then his shoulders slumped, and Laura knew he had given up. "I'll get my coat," he said.

Laura followed him into the kitchen, where his coat hung on a peg, hoping for a word alone with him. But Walt was right on their heels.

"Have to keep an eye on this fellow," said Walt, "so's he doesn't try to run out the back door."

Before he left, Bert stopped in the front hall. "Lock the door, Laura," he advised. "And don't let anyone in. Pa and Abby will be home by morning."

"I'll be all right." Laura's mouth was dry, and it was difficult to talk.

After they had gone, she bolted the door. Lamp in hand, she climbed back to the bedroom, quickly rolled back the carpet, and lifted the trap door.

"Bert's gone," she told Martin. "They had a warrant to take him in for questioning."

Martin's eyes looked up at her with a mute appeal. Never before had she seen such an expression of despair.

He climbed out and carefully replaced the trap door and carpet.

"I'll be going," he said.

"You can't. You don't know the way."

"You can tell me."

Laura shook her head. "You'd never find the place alone. You'll just have to wait until tomorrow. Pa will be home then and he'll know what to do."

"But tonight the boat's coming. And my pappy is waiting."

"I know." Laura could understand his impatience and longing.

"Your uncle's coming," Martin reminded her. "The one who doesn't believe in helping slaves get away. I'll find the river — don't you worry."

Laura wondered what Uncle Daniel would do if he found out they were hiding an escaped slave. He would never forgive Pa, and he might go straight to the sheriff.

"I *have* to leave!" Martin sounded desperate. "I'd rather *die* than get sent back to my master."

Laura saw the anguish in his face and knew suddenly that it was up to her, now.

"You're right, Martin," she said slowly. "You'll have to leave tonight, but you can't go alone. You'd get lost and you'd never get to the house on the river in time. I'm going with you."

Martin's face showed such surprise that Laura almost laughed.

"I can do it," she said stoutly. "I know how to get to the Tryon house." She began to make plans. "We won't go on the road. The slave catchers will be out tonight, especially now that George, that other slave, has escaped."

Martin was mute, staring at her as if trying to decide if she had lost her mind.

"We'll go through the woods," Laura said. "We'll stay as close to the road as we dare, so as not to get lost. You'll need a warm jacket. I'll see if Bert has one that will fit you."

"I don't want to get you in trouble, Miss Laura." Martin looked more worried than at any time since she had first seen him.

"You don't need to worry about me," said Laura. "I'm not like some girls who've never done anything but cook and sew and play on the piano. My mother used to say I was a tomboy. I used to know every nut tree and berry patch for miles around." She looked down at her long dress and noticed a three-cornered hole in the skirt where a thorny branch in the woods had caught it.

All at once she realized what a difficult task lay ahead. She remembered how hard it had been to walk in her long skirts up the overgrown lane to Tryon's Folly by daylight. How could she expect to travel more than a mile around the edge of Lewiston, all the way to the river at night? She couldn't do it, and yet she had to.

"I know what I'll do!" she declared. "I'll wear a pair of Bert's pants!"

Taking the lamp with her, she ran to her brother's room, where a thorough search of the wardrobe and chest of drawers turned up an old brown shirt that was slightly large for her, plus Bert's Sunday pants and his school pants. Both were much too large, and besides, this trip through the woods and Tryon's cellars would ruin them. Her brother's work pants were downstairs in the shed, but she knew they were no smaller than his good trousers. It wouldn't help to wear pants that would trip her up just as her skirts would. Why couldn't she have grown as fast as Bert? By rights, she should be bigger than he.

Still carrying the lamp, she entered the small attic that opened off Bert's room. Several boxes and trunks were stored under the slanting roof. In the third box she opened, she found exactly what she needed — Bert's clothes he'd worn as a boy — a pair of black pants and a jacket. She also took out a coat that would fit Martin and a worn cap. Her own shoes would have to do. She'd put on her sturdiest pair.

Back in Bert's room, she proceeded to dress in his old clothes, buttoning the jacket over Bert's brown shirt for warmth. For a final touch, she set his cap at a jaunty angle and tucked her long hair under it. A glance in the mirror showed her a mischievous face with big, excited eyes. She felt more alive than she had for years.

When she appeared in the doorway to her room, she was satisfied to see Martin's look of surprise and to hear the ring of truth in his voice as he said, "For a minute I thought you *were* a boy."

Time began to race. The moon was dropping lower in the sky, and as soon as it was out of sight, they must be ready to leave.

Laura filled a lantern with Potter's oil and stuffed several lucifers into a pocket of the jacket. Then, leaving a lamp burning on her dresser, she and Martin hurried from room to room, looking out of the windows on all sides of the house to see if anyone was lurking in the shadows.

Just as she had begun to hope that the slave catchers had stopped watching the house, Martin called out softly from her parents' room. She reached the front window in time to see a man saunter past on the road. Even without the moon's light, she could see that his head was turned toward the house. A few minutes later, he came back again, walking in the same measured way.

"We'll have to watch him, and leave the moment he's out of sight," said Laura.

Putting out the light, she led the way down the stairs in the dark. In the pitch-black kitchen, she stumbled against a chair. If she couldn't find her way across her own kitchen, how could she make her way through the woods she had not been in for four years? Quietly she opened the back door.

"Stay close to me," she whispered to Martin. "We'll head for that tree." She pointed to a large maple that stood half-way between the house and the woods. "If anyone shouts at us, just keep going. Never mind about me, just run!" She made a slow, careful survey of the yard. Nothing moved and there was no sound.

Someone could be hiding in the orchard to the right of the yard or in the woods toward which she planned to run, but that was a chance she would have to take.

"Do you see anyone?" she asked.

"No," answered Martin.

"Keep watching while I look for our sentry." She ran to the parlor and waited until the man stalked by and disappeared to the east. She raced back to the kitchen. "Now!" she panted.

Laura sprinted across the lawn and Martin followed her.

Flight by Night

As she ran toward the woods, Laura's first
thought was how easy it was to run without
skirts. Boys were certainly lucky.

Martin reached the shadow of the maple
tree almost as soon as she did. There they
paused. She was about to make a dash for
the woods, when she heard the clop-clop of a
horse's hoofs on the road. A horse and rider
came into view from the direction of Lewiston. Soon they were joined by the sentry
Laura had seen patrolling the road in front
of the house. Scarcely breathing, she and
Martin waited while the men talked, looking
often toward the Eastman house. If the men
glanced toward the back yard, would they
see the two who were standing in the shadow
of the maple? Laura thought not. She and
Martin were wearing dark clothes and Martin had the added advantage of a dark-

skinned face. Moving cautiously, she pulled her cap low over her forehead and lifted the collar of the jacket to hide as much as possible of her white skin.

After the longest five minutes of her life, the men parted — the one on horseback traveling toward Lewiston, and the other walking east.

As soon as the sentry's back was turned, she and Martin fled toward the woods.

Once under the cover of the trees, Laura paused to catch her breath.

"Stay close to me," she warned Martin again. "We mustn't get separated. Hang onto the back of my jacket."

She started forward slowly with the lantern in one hand and holding the other hand outstretched. A branch scraped harshly across her face and she came to a sudden halt, clutching her cap to keep from losing it. Martin, close on her heels, bumped into her.

"I can't see a thing!" she whispered. "I wish I dared light this lantern."

"Let me carry it," Martin suggested. "Then you can use two hands to fight off those branches."

They started forward again.

It was easier, Laura found, now that she had both hands free. Also, as time went on, her eyes became more accustomed to the dark, and soon she could see the black trunks of maple and beech and oak and the furry clumps of pine and spruce. She began to regain the confidence she'd once had when in the woods. Now and then a slight tug on the back of her jacket told her that Martin was with her.

The Ridge Road was on their left, and from the start, she had tried to bear in that direction. By now she should have reached it. Were they lost already? Surely not — not in these woods she had once known so well. Then, to her relief, she heard the rumble of carriage wheels not far off. Martin pulled at her jacket and she knew he, too, had heard the carriage.

Moving toward the sound, she saw ahead of her the white band of the road, gleaming dimly in the starlight. Seconds later a horse and carriage came into view, traveling at a quick pace. Even in the faint light Laura recognized the horse. It was Sally. Someone was on the carriage seat, leaning forward to urge the horse on, but Laura couldn't make out his features.

The carriage passed the two hiding in the woods, and Laura was about to move on when a horse and rider came pell-mell down the road after the carriage. She heard the rider shout, "'Allo! Where are you going?"

A voice answered from the carriage, "Down the road a piece. What business is it of yours?"

"That looks to me like the Eastman carriage — the one that kidnaped the runaway this afternoon."

"That it is," the man in the carriage admitted. "It turned up on Center Street not half an hour ago, so the sheriff asked me if I'd take it back where it belongs."

"No one's home at the Eastman place but the girl, and she's asleep. Sam's been watching the house ever since young Bert was picked up. The light went out in her room some time back."

Sam must be the sentry who had been patrolling the road in front of the house, Laura decided.

"I heard about Bert," said the man in the carriage. "Well, I'll put this rig in the barn and give the horse a bag of oats. No need to wake the girl."

Laura leaned against a tree, waiting while the horse and rider cantered past on their way back to Lewiston.

Martin whispered, "Too bad we can't get that carriage and ride to the river."

"I wish we could, but we're safer in the woods." Too many people were abroad tonight, Laura thought. The carriage would surely be stopped before they could reach Tryon's Folly.

"I know," Martin agreed. "Well, we'd better move on."

Keeping the Ridge Road in sight on the left, they pushed ahead, making good time until they neared a farmhouse. At their approach the farmer's dog set up such a racket that his owner came outside to investigate.

The dog ran directly toward the woods where Laura and Martin were standing, afraid to stir lest the crackle of dry leaves and branches betray them still further.

They could hear the man call, "Come back here, Rupert! I'm not chasing after any porcupines or skunks tonight!"

But Rupert was persistent, and finally the farmer gave in, saying, "All right. You win. I'll get my gun."

Hearing this, Laura and Martin waited only until the farmer entered the house for his gun. Then they ran as fast as they could.

In spite of her fright, Laura tried to keep her bearings. Their only hope was to stay in sight of the road. Although her memory of the land around Lewiston was coming back to her, she knew she couldn't find her way deep in the woods at night.

The barking of the dog proved to be a guide as well as a spur, for it helped Laura to lead the way in a wide circle around the farm. She and Martin pushed on until they fell to the ground, completely out of breath.

When the pounding of blood in her ears stopped, Laura listened for the dog, but silence had descended on the woods.

"Now I know how you felt with the bloodhounds after you," she told Martin.

"They're worse," he said. "They make that awful howling noise, and you know they never give up."

Martin sat up and examined the lantern, to which he had clung all through their wild flight. "It's still whole," he said.

Laura struggled slowly to her feet and walked unsteadily to the edge of the nearby clearing. "We've come around to the north of Lewiston," she said. "Mohawk Street is over there." She pointed to the left. "So if we go straight ahead, we should reach the river." She didn't want Martin to guess how worried she was. The trip was taking longer than she had expected. What if the boat had already come and gone by the time they reached Tryon's Folly?

In a few minutes they came onto the River Road, across from Judge Stow's estate. Laura felt encouraged. This last part of their trip had gone quickly.

"We're almost there," she said softly.

"Praise be," answered Martin.

They hurried north in the shelter of the trees, for Laura did not dare to cross the road at this point. Judge Stow's land was too open for safety.

When the dark mass of woods near Tryon's Folly lay opposite them, she whispered, "We'll cross here."

The road was empty in both directions, so she scurried over with Martin beside her. They had barely reached the other side when hoofbeats clattered out of the drive at Judge Stow's and came down the road toward Tryon's Folly. Martin dropped to the ground and lay motionless, while Laura crouched beside him.

Now the horse and rider were approaching more slowly. Laura could see a piebald horse and atop him the tall shape of Walt. Had he seen them dash across the road?

To Laura's relief, Walt continued down the road. With a whispered word to Martin, she stood up. Stepping cautiously, she led the way through the thick undergrowth until they reached the comparative openness of the lane. Here she paused to listen, and with dismay and fear, she heard the crashing sound of someone hurrying through the woods behind them. Walt must have seen them, after all.

Laura could think of only one thing. She must get Martin to the river before the slave hunter caught up with them.

"Come on!" she urged.

Martin obeyed, and in two or three minutes they burst out of the woods into the narrow clearing around Tryon's Folly.

Without a backward glance, Laura ran headlong toward the house. Martin's feet pounded after her, and together they dashed into the parlor. Bats whirred over their heads so close that Laura could feel the air stirred by their flight, but she had no time to be afraid of mere winged creatures. By the dim light that came through the high windows, she rushed through the rooms to the kitchen.

She flung open the door to the cellar. "Here are the stairs. Put your hand on the railing."

The darkness seemed to reach up to smother them. Laura felt as if she were descending into a well.

Behind her, Martin gasped, "Where are you?"

"Here." She tried to sound calm. "Give me the lantern."

She placed it on the floor, pulled a lucifer from her pocket, and struck it. In the flare she could see to open the lantern and touch the wick with the flame. She jumped to her feet, crossed to the door in the west wall, and then pulled it toward her. Ahead lay the short tunnel that sloped down to the next cellar.

"Come on!" She started ahead with the light. "Watch out for the stairs at the end of the tunnel."

"Yes, Miss Laura," said Martin.

Laura heard both fear and bravery in his voice. "Just a little farther," she encouraged him. "You'll soon be crossing the river."

They were in the second cellar, and Martin had the trap door raised when Laura, pausing to listen, heard a door open some place upstairs. Footsteps thudded far overhead. It sounded as if more than one person was up there. Walt must have a deputy or another slave catcher with him.

Laura exchanged a terrified glance with Martin. "Close the trap door, and hurry!" She plunged down the steps, stumbling and almost falling in her haste. Frantic with excitement, she glanced desperately around the third cellar. Where *is* that trap door? she asked herself. Only this afternoon she had been through these cellars, but now in her panic, she couldn't recall where the entrance to the next cellar was.

Martin snatched the lantern from her hand and scurried around the room. In a moment he had located the trap door in the floor, beneath the windows that faced the river.

Swiftly he raised the door, set the lantern on the floor, and stood aside, waiting for Laura.

"Go ahead," she whispered. "Down there you'll find a door on the side of the cellar toward the river. Run out and hide!"

Martin scrambled down the ladder, while Laura seized the lantern and turned to climb down after him.

Her foot found the top rung of the ladder and she reached for the trap door. To her horror she heard footsteps enter the room she was leaving. She had no time to lower the door.

Below her Martin warned, "Watch out for the last rung. It's loose."

Directly above her head someone asked, "Is that you, Martin?"

Surprised, Laura looked up into a dazzling light.

The person who was holding the lantern asked in a puzzled tone, "Laura?"

Such relief flooded through Laura that she almost lost her hold on the ladder. The man in the cellar was Joel Todd!

The Promised Land

Laura hastily resumed her descent and quickly reached the floor of the last cellar. "Martin! Wait!" she cried.

But the door onto the river bank was wide open, and Martin had disappeared into the darkness.

Suddenly a strong hand seized Laura's arm and swung her around. Holding his lantern so its light shone on her face, Joel demanded, "Laura, what are you doing here?" His eyes were fierce and probing.

Laura met his gaze defiantly. "Bert was arrested so I brought Martin here. This *is* the right place, isn't it?"

She was not prepared for Joel's reaction. He set the lantern on the damp floor of the cellar and wrapped his arms around her. "Laura, Laura!" he murmured. Then he began to chuckle. He held her off and searched her face again. "The rabbit in the trap!" he said, still smiling. "You couldn't bear to see Martin get caught, could you?"

"He's not safe yet!" Laura twisted away, and skirting the pool of water, ran outdoors. Below her lay the steep slope of the river bank, thickly covered with trees and shrubs. "Martin," she called softly. "It's all right! Joel's here."

A clump of bushes between her and the river stirred, and Martin came out.

Joel went to him and put his hand on his shoulder. "So Laura took care of you?"

"Yes, Mr. Joel. She brought me here through the woods without getting us lost once."

A loud splash and an exclamation made all three of them whirl around.

Joel picked up the lantern and in two long steps was again in the cellar doorway. "George!" he exclaimed. "I forgot about you. What happened?"

The fugitive whom Laura had seen outside the church emerged from the cellar. He sounded amused as he said, "I stepped in that pool."

"No wonder," Joel said apologetically. "I went off with the lantern."

George didn't seem upset. "No harm done. Just a wet foot."

Joel pulled a watch from his pocket and studied it by the light of the lantern. "It's time for your ride to the Promised Land," he said to George and Martin. "Let's get down to the shore quickly." He held out his left hand. "Come on, Laura."

Laura hesitated. "Walt — he's one of the slave catchers — was on the road a few minutes ago. He may have followed us here."

Joel stopped. "I doubt it. I saw him heading back toward Lewiston. But just to be sure, we'll put out the lanterns. We don't need them. I could find my way in my sleep."

Laura took his hand and started down the bank, though she still felt uneasy. Who could tell what Walt would do? He might have been pretending he was going to Lewiston, and in reality was planning to come back and surprise them.

She stepped on a loose stone and shuddered as it went rolling down the bank ahead of her. Was Walt up there listening? Well, even if he is, she thought grimly, he's too late to stop Martin and George.

Now the swift rush of the river reached her ears. The water here was deep and the current was powerful. Anyone who fell in would not survive for very long.

"Be careful," she warned Martin. "Don't get too close to the edge."

Joel led them to a large rock near the water and dropped onto it, drawing Laura down beside him. George and Martin stood to one side, talking quietly.

"You said they arrested Bert," Joel said. "Why'd they do that?"

"On suspicion," Laura told him. "It was our carriage that picked up George."

"Oh, of course. Now I see. Josiah Tryon told me one of our agents borrowed it. He knew Sally could outrun any other horse for miles around. But they can't prove Bert did anything wrong. Anyway, the judge is on our side. He just has to pretend to go along with the slave catchers."

"Then Mr. Tryon *is* in the Underground Railroad," Laura said. "Bert thought he was."

Joel nodded. "He's a fine man — the backbone of our operation in Lewiston. He and his wife spend their lives helping other people in all kinds of ways."

"How did you get out? This afternoon you were being guarded like a prisoner."

"The men finally gave up watching our house, and the minute they left, I went to Josiah and asked him what I could do. He told me where to find George and asked me to take him to meet the boat that was coming for Martin."

"Does Josiah Tryon own this house now?"

"No, his brother Amos still does. But it was Josiah who had the idea of using it as the Lewiston terminal of the Underground Railroad. Amos agreed with the plan." Joel rose and stared upstream. "I think the boat's coming."

Laura looked, too, and saw a rowboat gliding toward them in the deep shadow of the bank. In a few minutes, Joel and George leaped down to the water's edge, seized the bow of the boat, and pulled it against the shore.

Martin started after them, but then he turned around and came back to Laura. "Thank you, Miss Laura. I can't ever thank you enough."

Laura took his hand. All at once she had many things she wanted to say, but there was no time. "Send word to us where you are and we'll come to see you," she told him earnestly. "We'll be helping other slaves to cross the river, too."

She stood beside Joel, watching the boat start across the dark river. George and Martin waved, and then, as if drawn by a magnet, they turned their faces toward Canada.

"In a few minutes they'll be free," said Joel. "When they pass the middle of the river, they're in Canadian waters."

"I hope they'll be all right," said Laura. "Martin is such a young boy to have traveled so far alone."

"He's safe now. His father will be on the shore to meet him." Joel took Laura's elbow. "How am I going to get you home in that outfit?"

They climbed up the river bank before they again lighted the lanterns. With Joel beside her, Laura found that the dark, empty cellars of Tryon's Folly were no longer places of terror.

To Laura's surprise, after they closed the front door behind them, Joel did not head for the lane through the woods. Instead, he took her arm and said, "I want to show you something."

Mystified, she let him lead her to the narrow terrace behind the house. There he pushed aside a curtain of wild grapevine and stopped at a huge boulder. Dropping Laura's hand, he set his lantern on the ground, leaned against the stone, and with a great effort pushed it aside.

Laura was amazed to see that the boulder had concealed an opening in the ground. Joel lowered his lantern into the hole, and Laura, dropping to her knees, stared into a rock-walled room the size of the pantry at home, with a vaulted stone ceiling.

"This is where the slaves hide while they're waiting for a boat to take them to Canada," Joel explained. "I think it was built for use as a cistern to hold rain water, but it makes a good hiding place. Only the Tryons, my father and yours, and I know about this." He paused. "And now you know."

Grateful for his trust in her, Laura said, "Thank you for showing me. Bert and I thought there should be a safer place than the cellars." She had a sudden notion. "Joel! This is where the men brought George after they picked him up at the church this afternoon!"

Joel laughed. "You're a smart one. Yes, he stayed here until I came after him tonight." He returned the stone to its place. "Last night, on account of the dogs, I couldn't bring Martin here. Anyway, he needed just what he had at your house — food and warmth and friends to talk to."

They went down the lane, putting out their lanterns before they reached the River Road.

Joel had worked out a plan.

"We'll go back to my house, and if anyone sees us on the way, we'll hope they think we're just a couple of boys out for a late walk. Mother will fix you a bed for the rest of the night."

"Thank you," said Laura. "That would be fine, but I must go home. Pa and Abby — and Uncle Daniel — will be back from Buffalo very early in the morning and they'll be worried if they don't find Bert or me at home."

At Joel's house, Mrs. Todd gave Laura a skirt to pull over her trousers and a cloak that covered the entire outfit.

Laura came into the kitchen wrapped in the cloak, but still wearing Bert's cap.

"How do I look now?" she asked Joel.

He laughed. "Almost like a girl." In a flash he whipped off the cap and her dark blond hair tumbled onto her shoulders. "Now you're yourself again." His eyes told her that was the way he liked her.

Joel then said he had the horse and buggy waiting in front of the house.

"You don't have to take me," she said. "I can walk home."

"Child, child," said Mrs. Todd. "You must be exhausted!"

Laura considered this. "I am tired."

Mrs. Todd kissed her cheek. "It's a brave thing you did tonight."

Was I brave? Laura wondered. She had done what she had to do. That was all. Of two things she was sure — after tonight's business she knew where she belonged and which side she was on. She had come home to stay.

Laura and Joel were at the edge of town when Walt and his horse came clattering down Center Street after them.

"Hold on there, young Todd!" he called out. "Who's that with you?" He leaned closer. "Laura Eastman!" He began to laugh derisively. "So you gave us all the slip and went out for a buggy ride. I didn't know you had a sweetheart."

Laura would have protested, but Joel said, "That she has," and drew his arm tight around her shoulders.